THE
GILL MAN
IN
PURGATORY

THE GILL MAN IN PURGATORY

stories by

David Denny

SHANTI ARTS PUBLISHING

BRUNSWICK, MAINE

THE GILL MAN IN PURGATORY

Published by Shanti Arts Publishing
Cover and interior design by Shanti Arts Designs

Shanti Arts LLC
Brunswick, Maine
www.shantiarts.com

Printed in the United States of America

First edition
10 9 8 7 6 5 4 3 2 1

ISBN: 978-1-941830-75-8 (softcover)
ISBN: 978-1-941830-76-5 (digital)

LCCN: 2015949898

For Paul Morgan Stetler, who knows why or should.

Contents

Acknowledgments

Grateful acknowledgment is made to the editors of the following publications in which these stories first appeared, some in slightly different versions:

Celery, "Not Talking About the Moon"
Clare, "The Gill Man in Purgatory"
A Clean, Well-Lighted Place, "Hemingway's Juvenalia"
Main Street Rag, "Here, Alfred Hitchcock"
New Ohio Review, "Coins for the Ferryman"
Pearl, "Like You Don't Really Care" and "The View from Molokai"
Pilgrim, "Pillar Saint"
Relief, "Who Could Hang a Name on You?"
The Sand Hill Review, "The Art of Divination"
Stoneboat, "Inheriting the Earth"
Stone Voices, "Gravidation" and "The Haiku Master's Wife"

It is good that you should take hold of the one,
without letting go of the other.
— Ecclesiastes 7:18

Coins for the Ferryman

MARLENE AND RALPH walked up Kaanapali Beach about half a mile from their hotel. They sat in a corner of an outdoor restaurant with a floor of sand. Each of the small, round tables was shaded by an umbrella made of palm leaves. A row of tropical greenery, punctuated with orange and red hibiscus, separated the restaurant from the boardwalk. They could hear the waves hitting the sand about forty feet away.

Marlene slipped off her sandals and wiggled her toes in the cool sand as she looked over the menu. Mahi was her new favorite; however, she'd eaten it two days in a row and thought she should try something else. Up next to the bar, a local singer was nearing the end of his lunchtime set. He took a slug of water, traded his guitar for a ukulele, and began crooning the popular island version of "Somewhere Over the Rainbow." Marlene wasn't all that hungry. A shrimp cocktail and a Diet Coke might do the trick. Her husband had his cell phone out on the table in front of him, checking their reservation for the dinner cruise out of Lahaina harbor. He had decided before he left the hotel that he would order a burger; he was tired of fish already.

Marlene felt a tickle, like someone drawing a feather across the top of her left foot. Instinctively, she lifted her foot, shook it a little, and looked down to see if perhaps she had brushed up against her own sandal. Clinging to her foot was the ugliest thing she had ever seen outside a horror movie. She couldn't name it at that moment. But it looked and moved like a creature from a nightmare: about eight inches long, its brown and red segmented body had dozens of legs going every which way. The front part of it was fixed upon a spot at the base of her second toe and the rest of its body wriggled and crawled in several directions at once.

Marlene screamed and stood, knocking her chair into the next table. She tried to shake the thing off her foot. "Shit!" she screamed. Her husband saw her kicking her leg out in a weird hopping motion. He picked up her sandal from its place next to her chair and clipped the insect loose. It scurried across the sand and disappeared beneath the tropical plants next to their table.

The music stopped. People craned their necks to see the trouble. The elderly gentleman at the next table had been knocked over by the force of Marlene's chair. He was helped to his feet by his daughter, who was alternately lifting her father and trying to see what the man at the next table had been slapping at.

The waiter approached. "Is everything all right?"

"Oh my god!" Marlene cried. She sat heavily and cradled her foot in both hands. She rocked back and forth. Her face was red. She winced and wept. "You can't believe the . . . pain!" she cried. "Oh my god."

"Did it sting you?" Ralph asked.

"Oh my god!"

Those at the adjoining tables were on their feet, by turns looking at Marlene in her agony and searching the sand for the culprit, whatever it was.

Ralph turned to the waiter. "What kind of a place is this?"

"How can I help?" the waiter asked.

"Stop the pain," Marlene said.

The waiter looked at her foot, which was turning red now and beginning to swell. "Let me get you some ice," he said, hurrying towards the kitchen.

The hostess left her podium and stood in the middle of the restaurant, gawking. Someone tapped her on the shoulder. "We're moving over to the bar," a woman said.

Ralph knelt next to Marlene and examined her foot. "What was that thing?" he asked.

A young woman at the table next to Ralph said, "I saw it. It looked like a centipede."

"It was . . . huge," Ralph said.

"Everything grows bigger in this climate," the young woman said.

"Oh my god, Ralph, you can't believe how much this hurts!"

Some of the patrons began to leave the restaurant. In the process of packing his instruments, the singer knocked over his tip jar, sending a splash of coins across the electronic keyboard. Even people walking along the boardwalk stopped to see what had caused the commotion. Murmurs quickly turned to idle speculation. Sent to get the news, a teenager called down the boardwalk to his friends, "Some lady's purse got jacked."

The manager approached the table, followed by the waiter, who held some ice cubes in a plastic baggie. "Can you tell me what happened?" the manager asked.

Ralph relayed the story for the manager.

"I'm so, so sorry," the manager said. "I can assure you this has never happened before." He knelt next to Marlene while the family at the next table gathered their purses and snorkel kits. The woman who had come to the rescue of her elderly father said, "We've been coming to Hawaii for thirty years, and I've never even heard of anything like this before." She patted Marlene's shoulder with genuine compassion. "You take care now. Don't let this ruin your vacation." She and her party squeezed past the manager and the waiter and the hostess.

"May I?" The manager offered to examine Marlene's foot. He took her foot in his hand. She gasped and turned her head; the tendons in her neck strained.

"Look at that," Ralph said, pointing to two small puncture wounds at the base of her second toe. The top of her foot was bruised next to the wounds and her foot was puffy and reddish.

"I'm just going to put some ice right here." He took the baggie from the waiter and placed it gently atop the puncture wounds. "Now, is that OK?"

The manager held the ice to Marlene's foot. She sat with her head in one hand and the other hand gripping the edge of the table. She tried to breathe as evenly as she could. She wasn't getting any relief from the pain, but she made an effort to accommodate the manager. The waiter had gone to soothe the nerves of customers at his other tables.

"Well," the manager forced a smile. "Most people who come to Maui go home with snorkeling stories about puffer fish or sea turtles. You'll have something unique to share around the water cooler."

Ralph asked, "Any relief yet?"

Marlene pushed the ice off her foot. "That's only making it worse."

The manager stood. "Let me know if I can do anything."

"Do you want to head back to the hotel?" Ralph asked. "Maybe lie down awhile?"

"Oh my god, Ralph. Did you ever see anything so ugly?"

"That was truly disgusting."

"I don't see any point in sitting here," she said. "I can't eat anything now. Oh, shit, Ralph. Shit, shit, shit!" She picked up her sandals and her purse and clutched them in one hand. She took a deep breath and reached for Ralph's hand. "Get me out of here."

Ralph tucked his cell phone into his pocket and helped Marlene to her feet. She hobbled through the sand, each step on the left foot stabbed her, as if a paring knife were inserted between tarsal bones. People kindly moved chairs aside and wished her well as the couple navigated across the restaurant and back around to the boardwalk. It took them half an hour to get back to the hotel. The pain and swelling grew worse. People stared and pointed and asked if they could help. "Jelly fish?" someone asked. Ralph called ahead to the hotel on his cell and asked that a doctor be sent to their room.

ONCE BACK INSIDE, Ralph got Marlene into a comfortable chair and propped her foot on the edge of a suitcase. Marlene's ankle was swollen now, as if it was sprained, and her foot continued to discolor. The reddish marks around the puncture wounds were now blue as bruises.

"You just can't believe how much this hurts," she cried. "This is more intense than childbirth. I mean, I know it's just my foot but, holy shit, it's like it's on fire!"

"Maybe we should try the ice again."

"Fuck the ice! I didn't stub my toe, I was stung by god-knows-what."

"You're really starting to sweat," Ralph said. "Let me turn the AC up."

"Where's that doctor?" Marlene asked.

"They said they would call him and give him our room number. Do you want me to take you to the hospital?"

"I don't know. Do I need to go to the hospital? Was that thing as poisonous as it was ugly?"

"Strange that such a small creature could have such a harsh sting — "

"Small?!"

"I mean, you know, relatively speaking."

"It was as big as a banana!" She reached down and massaged her calf. "All right, now it's pretty much my whole leg that hurts. What the hell is this?"

Ralph looked at her, helpless. He wanted to stop the pain somehow. It was true he didn't love Marlene anymore — at least, not in the way he once had. But he didn't want her to suffer. He had lived with her for almost forty years. In a sense, the marriage had dried up in the last decade; however, they still treated one another with affection and a level of civility that they didn't see in many other couples their age. They had avoided the nasty public snipes and behind-the-back complaints that characterized so many of their friends' marriages.

There was a knock at the hotel room door. Ralph let the doctor in. As he entered the room, the doctor peeled from his face a pair of small, round sunglasses that looked like black half-dollars. He was a tall, deeply-tanned, sandy-blonde man of about thirty-five, right around their daughter's age. He wore a faded blue t-shirt atop his khaki shorts. He might have looked just as natural carrying a surfboard as a medical bag. Immediately, Ralph noticed something odd about his face, his mouth, but in his stressed state he couldn't pin it down. The young doctor set his black medical bag on the edge of the bed while Marlene and Ralph told him their story.

The doctor examined her foot, noting the puncture wounds and the swelling in her foot and ankle. He spoke with an Australian accent. "Yeah, these giant centipedes can be nasty. They're really a pain when they nest next to the house. They like dark, moist areas. They've been known to crawl in through bathroom fixtures. There was a guy up in Kula who got bit while taking a shower. The thing came right up through the drain. They keep the local pest control guys in business, that's for sure. You can kill them with insecticide, but that's all. They're impervious to everything else. You can chop them up and they'll still wiggle on their ghoulish way."

"Are they poisonous?" Ralph asked.

"Well, they inject venom, yeah. That's how they kill their prey, which is usually spiders and worms and other centipedes."

"They eat other centipedes?" Ralph asked.

"They're nasty little buggers," the doctor said. "You're the first tourist to get bit that I know of. There must be a nest in the plants there on the edge of the restaurant. Usually they only come out at night. Maybe this one's developed an appetite for the local cuisine," he said, smiling.

At the smile, Ralph realized what was different about the doctor's face: he had a small blonde goatee just beneath his lower lip. What was it they called those things? Ralph focused his attention — ah, yes, it was called a soul patch.

"Is there some sort of tropical ointment for this?" Marlene asked. "Because I gotta tell you, this hurts like a sonuvabitch."

He shook his head. He pulled a few things from his medical bag. He took Marlene's blood pressure. "Just try to relax and breathe normally," he said.

"Yeah, that's not gonna happen," Marlene said. She twisted her behind in the chair and rubbed her thigh. Despite the air conditioning, her brow was sweaty. She had developed a bit of a tan the past two days; however, now her face looked pale.

"Your BP's a little high," he said, tearing the Velcro wrap from her arm.

Marlene reached down and took hold of her foot. "OK, now my foot is numb," she said. "My foot is numb and the pain is going up my leg."

The doctor moved the stethoscope to her heart. He listened for a moment. "Do you have a heart murmur?" he asked.

"No."

He stood and wrapped the stethoscope into a ball, returning it to his bag.

"Can an insect bite affect the heart?" Ralph asked.

"Take a slow, deep breath," he said.

When she couldn't get a deep breath, Marlene grabbed Ralph's hand. The doctor picked up the room telephone and called for an ambulance.

BY THE TIME Marlene arrived at the ER, her leg was numb up to her knee and her thigh was throbbing with pain. She was receiving IV fluids; an epinephrine syringe lay on a tray next to her bed in case the pain or numbness advanced to her torso. The nurse had been given instructions to stab her thigh with the epi syringe if the patient's lips turned blue or if she grabbed her throat to signal choking.

Outside the room, Ralph reported what he could remember of Marlene's medical history to the Indian doctor who had taken her case. The doctor seemed especially interested in any allergies she might have, especially to bees. "Sometimes an allergy to one kind of insect venom indicates a tendency towards another. You are sure she is not allergic to bee stings?"

"No, I'm not sure," Ralph answered. "I don't think she's ever been stung. Not since I've known her. But I think I would know. I think she would've told me, and I don't remember that she has *any* allergies, much less to bee stings. She's a total rock. She's never been sick a day in her life. The only time she's been in a hospital is when our daughter was born."

"All right. That is a good sign."

"Can you give her something for the pain?"

"I cannot give her anything right now until we see how far the numbness and pain proceed. If the numbness advances into her torso, then we are into a different kind of situation."

"What kind of a situation?"

"Let's not get ahead of ourselves. Right now, she is in pain, I know, and she is panicked. But if I can get her to relax and if the progress of the numbness stops, then I will be able to give her something. Already I've given her an antihistamine. Let's give that a few minutes."

"And in a few minutes?"

"It may be necessary to start her on a steroid treatment."

"Is that the standard protocol for a giant centipede bite?"

"There is no standard protocol beyond the antihistamine. This is a very rare reaction your wife is having. Most people don't experience symptoms beyond pain and swelling around the puncture wound. Beyond the antihistamine, we are making the treatment up as we go along. I did a quick Google search as your wife was being transported. There is only one other case like this in the literature."

"Only one other rare reaction, you mean?"

"In one young man on Oahu two years ago, the ER staff reported an acute myocardial infarction brought on by the bite of a giant Scolopendra."

Ralph spoke the words mechanically: "A heart attack."

"He survived. Right now, I am more concerned about your wife's lung function. If her shortness of breath advances, it might be a sign of anaphylaxis."

"Then what?"

Then we are at a new code level."

"What should I do?"

"You mentioned a daughter. It might be a good idea to notify her. She should be apprised of the situation in case your wife's condition does not improve. But please go into the waiting room to call her. There is no need to alarm her; however, you should let her know what has happened."

Ralph walked down the hallway, through the heavy ER doors and into a waiting room with the usual chairs, magazines, and vending machine. A young boy sat sideways in his mother's lap, his thumb in his mouth. The woman looked vacantly out the window. In a corner of the room a flat-screened TV was playing infomercials for a variety of medical procedures. Ralph had seen them all before, in the waiting room of his internist back home. He found the remote control. "Do you mind?" he asked her, lifting the remote. She shook her head. Ralph clicked the mute button.

MARLENE LAY FLAT on her back with a moist towel across her forehead. The nurse was applying adhesive patches with wires to her chest and arms and legs. She would soon plug these all into a heart monitor. The pain in her leg had begun to subside. The doctor didn't know why; that is, he wasn't sure if that meant that the numbness was advancing or if the venom had run its course. He and the nurses were clearly mystified by her symptoms. They had all seen insect bites before, but nothing like this. They were polite and deliberate in their actions. Mostly they watched her. She hated being the latest "interesting case" in the ER. She was a person, with a history, a life, a family that depended upon her. And even though her husband had acted like a nincompoop lately, she loved him. Where had he gone anyway? The doctor had guided him into the hallway when they began applying the heart monitor, but now the thing was up and running, beeping and sending little lines across a screen. The doctor was there but Ralph was gone.

The doctor seemed pleased with the results the heart monitor was giving them. He shone a light into her eyes. He took hold of her wrist. "Things are looking up," he said, smiling. "I think that nasty centipede has done its worst."

"Where's my husband?" she asked.

"Forgive me, I sent him on a small errand. He will be back soon."

The doctor said this with an air of confidence. Whereas Marlene would not hesitate to ask for more details from a white doctor, she felt a bit intimidated by this Indian man, whose manner suggested superiority and cool detachment. What sort of a doctor sends his patient's spouse on an errand? What was Ralph doing? When she thought of the word *errand* she pictured Ralph pulling the garbage cans to the curb, walking the dog, or picking up the mail. She wanted him back at her bedside. Lately, he had a tendency to withdraw from her. He had disappeared for long stretches of the afternoon at home. Her Bunco friends had spotted him out walking, head down, hands shoved deep in his pockets. Newly retired, he didn't know what to do with himself. It was this tendency of his to withdraw from her that Marlene thought a trip to an exotic locale might reverse.

RALPH GOT THEIR daughter on the line and explained what had happened. He told her they were in the emergency room and that they were monitoring

Marlene's reaction to the centipede's venom. He tried to downplay the situation, but the daughter was upset.

"Should I fly there?" she asked.

"I think right now there isn't any point in that. This Indian doctor seems very sharp. He has a few tricks up his sleeve." Ralph did a poor imitation of an Indian accent. "He comes from a long line of snake charmers in Delhi." He smiled at the mother and son. The woman glared at him.

"Oh my god, dad," his daughter said. "That is so racist! Are you saying that with the doctor right there?"

"No. Of course not."

Ralph heard a siren in the distance, approaching the hospital from the opposite direction of Highway 30, the same road they had arrived by only twenty minutes earlier. He turned away from the mother and son and looked out the window.

"Mom would kill you if she heard that. Are you sticking by her?"

"I'm right here with her."

"Are you in the room with her?"

"I've been in the room with her. Right now they want me out of the way."

"Dad, don't leave her side. Go back in there with her."

"I will."

"Stay with her, dad."

"You don't need to tell me that."

"Daddy, sometimes you can be . . . aloof. She needs you near."

Ralph could see the ambulance approaching the hospital now. It was turning off the highway and coming up the access road towards the emergency entrance, lights and siren still going. Two police cruisers followed.

"Who are you calling aloof?" he asked.

"Let me talk to her."

"She's being treated right now."

"Just hold the phone up to her ear."

"I can't do that. They don't allow cell phones. They interfere with the fancy equipment. Later, when things have settled down. They're working on her right now."

"What does that mean — working on her?"

"They need her quiet right now. I'll call back in a little while after the antihistamine takes effect and then you can talk."

"I'm getting a flight."

"Look. I'm only calling to let you know what happened. She's going to be fine. It's crazy to book a flight right now. By the time you got here, we'd be packing to come back home." The ambulance approached the special turn-around at the back of the building. The sliding door of the hospital whooshed open; two nurses and a doctor in green scrubs emerged.

There was a long pause on the line. "Sylvie?" he said.

"Dad. I'm going crazy here." He could hear a quiver in her voice.

"Everything's going to be fine."

"I can't lose you two. You know how much I depend on you. I'm scared to death of losing you."

"Listen to me now. You're not losing us. Her. Or me. Nobody's losing anybody. It's just a bug bite. She's going to be fine."

"Go back to her side."

"I'm going back to check on her now. We . . . I just thought you should know what's going on, that's all. Other than this, we've had a good trip. Your mother swam with a sea turtle yesterday. She's having a blast. I'm going back to the exam room now. I'll call you later, OK?"

"As soon as you can."

"As soon as I can."

"Tell mom I love her."

"I'll tell her."

"I love you both."

"Love you, hon. Give our best to what's-his-name."

"That joke stopped being funny a long time ago. Derek and I have been married ten years."

"How did I get a daughter so old?" The ambulance backed up to the open doors. "Everything's fine. I'll — we'll call back in just a little while."

Ralph put the phone in his pocket and stood looking out the window. The siren pinched off in the middle of a whine. The back doors of the ambulance popped opened and the EMTs pulled the gurney out. An unconscious man lay under a white sheet, an oxygen mask covering his face. They hustled him inside. There but for fortune, thought Ralph. He had felt the odd pain in his chest lately — more than the usual aches and pains — and wondered how much time he had before he was the man on the gurney.

Ralph turned back to look at the mother and her son. The boy was asleep. She was stroking his hair and humming a soft tune in his ear. Ralph gestured towards the TV. "Do you want me to turn the sound back on?"

"My husband is Indian," she said.

"Oh. I didn't mean anything racial by that. I was trying to keep my daughter calm. You see, we're going through a stressful time here, and I was trying to keep things light." The look on the woman's face told Ralph that he was not going to be able to justify himself. People are so serious these days. They take things like this so literally. Sylvie did, too. Young people, he thought, they don't know how to laugh anymore.

"I need to sit for a moment. Do you mind?" He took a seat beneath the TV. He glanced over at the magazines on the table next to him. They were all celebrity stories and storm news. There had always been gossip rags around, but he wondered about the whole global warming thing. Since when was the occasional hurricane a sign of looming apocalypse? He had grown up shoveling snow six months a year in Wisconsin. Weather was just weather, he thought. No need to get excited. Deal with it, folks.

Noticing the vending machine on the opposite side of the room, he stood and fished through his pockets for change. He squinted at the machine. "Since when do they charge a buck and a quarter for a Diet Coke?" He approached the vending machine counting the change in his palm. "It was two bits for a Coke just yesterday. Yesterday being nineteen-hundred-and-fifty-five." He smiled at the woman; she turned away.

He put the coins into the slot. "The Hawaiian fellow who drives the little tourist train from Kaanapali to Lahaina told us that these hills back here used to be covered with sugar cane." Ralph sang a bit of the old commercial jingle: "C & H. Pure cane sugar. From Hawaii. Growin' in the sun." His can of Diet Coke dropped with a loud thud into the dispenser. The boy startled in his mother's lap. "Oh, sorry," Ralph said. "So sorry." The boy turned to one side and sucked harder on his thumb, eyes still closed.

Ralph opened his can and took a sip. He looked out the window again. The black and green hills that rose up above Lahaina were lined with deep, shadowed ridges of moist basalt. The afternoon sun accentuated the texture of the mountains as they rose steeply above the backside of the hospital. Somewhere up out of his view was a dormant volcano. The bell boy at the hotel had told him the name of it on the day of their arrival, but he couldn't remember. It wasn't Haleakalā — that was down in the lower half of the island. This one wasn't as high, but it was partly responsible for the birth of this island, nevertheless — the valley island, Hawaiians called it.

They had planned a dinner cruise for this evening, on a ship that went up and down the coastline of west Maui. He would have had to eat seafood, yes, but there would also have been live music — a jazz combo — and an open bar. Probably right now, down at the dock, they were readying the boat. If not for that damned centipede, they would've been sipping Mai Tais this evening while taking their seats at a table on the bow. Ah, well. *C'est la vie.* It was a phrase he repeated to himself often. *C'est la vie.* It was the only French he knew.

Ralph wondered what might happen if he walked out of the hospital right now and kept walking. How hard would it be to lose yourself on such an island? What would happen if he took all the cash he could get from the ATM, left his wallet with his credit cards and his ID, all his luggage and his cell phone too in the hotel room, and launched out on a new life? The bell boy had told him you could live cheaply upcountry — that was the local word for the small towns that dotted the slopes of Haleakalā at the two-to-four-thousand foot level. He could find a job in a coffee shop or a bookstore, live simply, take walks everyday along the ridges overlooking the Au'au Channel. Start over. He wouldn't need much. He would grow a soul patch. Maybe even get a tattoo. Nothing too fancy, just one of the island designs he saw wrapped around the arms of the young men in Lahaina Town. Hell, he might meet a local woman and set up house with her in a small cottage surrounded by tropical flowers. Vegetables must sprout easily and grow year-round in the rich, volcanic soil. He could see himself growing old gracefully here, with dignity and freedom. The guidebook said people lived longer in Hawaii because of lower stress levels, surrounding beauty, warm climate, and the clean, fresh environment.

One of the nurses from the ER poked her head in the door of the waiting room. "Your wife's asking for you," she said.

Ralph nodded. He looked at the young mother and her son. He thought maybe he should apologize. But what for? For being himself? He had offended her somehow. He had disturbed her. If she would just return his gaze, he might think of the right words to say. The nurse was holding the door for him.

MARLENE HAD TAKEN Ralph's hand as soon as he returned to her side. She would not let go. She was breathing easier now. The doctor wanted to keep her plugged into the monitor for twenty-four hours, even though he was confident that she was out of danger. He had given her some hydrocodone for the pain. He had consulted by telephone with a neurologist in Honolulu. He would begin a regimen of steroids, in a slowly ascending dosage, until the swelling subsided. He believed the feeling would return to her leg in a few days time. He had moved on to other patients now; however, the doctor wanted to interview Marlene later, take some further notes on her case; it might make an interesting paper for the *Emergency Medicine Journal*.

"I always knew you'd be famous," Ralph said.

"I'd rather be famous as a dancer."

"You were doing some pretty fine tap moves there in the sand." He drew a smile from her when he imitated her spastic movements in the restaurant.

"We can never go there again."

"I think we should, and we should bring that manager a big bag of ice as a reward for his heroism."

Ralph pulled his cell phone from his pocket and called their daughter. He handed Marlene the phone. "Tell Sylvie you're all right," he said. "She was this close to getting on a plane."

She held the phone to her ear. "Hi hon . . . I'm fine, I'm fine," Marlene began.

Ralph slipped out the door while Marlene spoke to Sylvie. He walked down the hallway. The waiting room was empty now. He wandered a bit, peeking into exam rooms. In one of them he saw the Indian doctor speaking to a young man with his shirt off. He was showing the doctor a bright red rash on his shoulder. In another he saw a table on wheels loaded with all sorts of electronic equipment. Ralph thought it resembled an old ham radio set. Edging up to the doorframe, he could see the tubes and wires snaking behind a curtain. He pushed the curtain aside. The tubes and wires ran up beneath the covers of the man on the gurney, the one who had arrived in the ambulance after them. The man's vacant eyes stared up at the ceiling. A clear plastic tube stuck out of his mouth. Where was this man's doctor? Why had the nurses abandoned him? Ralph stood for a moment before he realized he was looking at a corpse. He stepped further into the room, pulled the curtain behind him, and stood beside the gurney.

The wreckage of machinery and packaging scattered about the room suggested that they had worked hard to revive the man. In the end, someone had switched off the equipment, lowered the lights, and gone to notify his next of kin, if he had any. This had all happened while Ralph and Marlene were down the hall celebrating that she was not going to die today.

He wasn't sure if he should, but Ralph felt compelled to touch the man. He rested his hand upon the man's exposed arm. It felt cool and rubbery. His body looked bloated beneath the sheet; his face was puffy and gray. It occurred to Ralph that the man had drowned. The eyes held their color, the same color as the ocean that had swallowed him, but they were blind eyes now. He remembered learning in school how the ancients used to place coins on the eyes of the dead. Why? Was it to pay their fare into the next life? Ralph passed his hand over the man's face, closing the eyes.

His own eyes began to blur; he felt a warmth rising within, as if a balm had been applied to his chest. The warm feeling spread across his shoulders and up into his throat. A whimper pushed through his lips. The strange heat of tears rolled down his cheeks. His shoulders began to heave. There was no stopping now. He had not cried since the day Sylvie was born. Standing at the deathbed of a stranger, he gave himself over to it. As if swept by a strong current, he relaxed his hold on himself and allowed his body to be taken by a hundred emotions that he had stifled for years, for decades.

There was a rustle in the hallway. The doctors and nurses were going about their business. Clutching a clipboard, a nurse abruptly moved the curtain aside, exposing Ralph in his grief, and then she drew it slowly back again, apologizing as she backed out. Perhaps she thought he was a relative, the man's brother, come to say his farewell. Over the intercom a woman's voice called a certain doctor to radiology. Murmurs and footsteps approached and receded. The elevator bell rang a single note of arrival. The Indian doctor spoke into the telephone at the desk, calling in a prescription. Down the hallway, Marlene assured her daughter that she would call her again once she was transferred to a regular room. A nurse injected an amber fluid into the tube of her IV. In the room next to her, a mother and her young son stood at the bedside of an elderly woman who had slipped into a coma earlier in the day.

Outdoors, the ambulance driver tossed his spent cigarette to the asphalt, stamping it beneath his boot. The radio in his unit crackled as a voice announced that he was needed at the Pineapple Inn, Kehei. Looming above him, the steep mountains of Mauna Kahalawai caught the full brilliance of the afternoon sun. And in the harbor below, the morning excursion boats returned, dock boys dragged hoses along the wharf, spraying down the decks, while the shorebirds hovered and called out for scraps. ∎

The View from Molokai

ROGER HAS GOT hold of me and won't let go. He's stopped crying, but the whole front of my game jersey is wet with his snot and tears. I'd rather not explain to the others in the ER waiting room why one grown man is clinging to another so desperately; luckily, nobody here seems particularly interested anyway. They've all got their own crises to deal with. There is a mother of a teenage gunshot victim in here with us. She is using a recent copy of *Cosmopolitan* magazine to keep her from imagining what her son is going through in the operating room. A homeless man was brought in growling like a rabid dog a few minutes ago. He stopped growling long enough to tell the nurses that he was possessed. Several others sit in the molded plastic chairs staring out the windows or up at the television screen, which is showing an old black-and-white movie with no sound. I've seen the movie before. Bette Davis has shot her lover and spends the whole movie pretending it was justifiable homicide. Only her gullible husband believes her. Right now she's kissing him even though you can tell she's disgusted by him, the poor sap. Up at the nurse's station window the roommate of a girl who was killed in a car accident this afternoon is giving the names and phone numbers of her next of kin from the dead girl's cell phone.

As for us, it was just about an hour ago that our friend, Lynda, was brought in here with a head injury. She seemed OK at first, but things have sure gone downhill fast. Roger is particularly upset because it was he who threw the softball at Lynda's forehead at close range, raising a knot roughly the size and shape of a plum right between her eyebrows. Despite the name, softballs are not especially soft. The 14-incher we use in the co-ed league can raise a welt if it misses your glove. I'd rather not describe the sound the ball made when it impacted poor Lynda's head this evening. The word thud doesn't begin to capture it.

Just after we arrived, the nurse told us Lynda had had a seizure during the ambulance ride. And right after they got her into a treatment room, she lost consciousness. If Lynda dies tonight, I suppose Roger will find it hard to live with himself. If Lynda dies tonight, I might just kill Roger.

IT WAS THE third inning. After hitting a nice blooper into left centerfield, Lynda was on first—that's my position, first base. Her teammate hit a grounder to short, a classic double play ball. Chin, our short stop, tossed it to Roger, who tagged his base and launched it toward me. But the ball never arrived. There was that sound of the impact that I refuse to describe, and then Lynda dropped to her knees in the middle of the base path, and then Lynda dropped to the ground. Pretty much immediately all the blood drained from Roger's face. Lynda was still conscious at this point.

Carol, who was playing in shallow right, yelled to Don, our catcher-manager, to get the ice pack out of the first aid kit. By the time I got to her, Lynda had already sprouted that plum. She was shaky and nauseous. So were we all. Carol called 911. Some of us took a knee and tried to make light conversation about the rather sizable bump on her forehead. Some just stood around looking queasy.

Lynda kept asking, "Am I out? I'm out, right? Did Roger tag the base?" She looked up at Roger. "Am I out?" He just stared back at the big purple lump on her forehead, sweat dripping down his face. Carol had the presence of mind to place the ice pack on her forehead and keep her still.

They pulled the ambulance right out onto the field, checked her pupils, checked her blood pressure, and loaded her into the back of the ambulance. As they slid her gurney in, she turned to me and asked, "Why won't anybody tell me if I'm safe or out?"

"I think you're safe," I said.

"Are you sure?" she said as they closed the doors. I could see through the rear window that she was carrying on this line of questioning with the EMT, who was looking for a good vein in which to insert an IV.

All of this seemed to take forever, the way things do when a traumatic event occurs. I once saw a car swerve at high speed on the freeway, spin out, then flip over four times. It was like watching a slow-motion movie. But in actuality time was plugging along as it always does. Pretty soon Lynda was on Mr. Toad's Wild Ride to the hospital, and we were left standing on the field looking at each other. I remember glancing down at the glove on my right hand and wondering what it was doing there. What the hell was this dirty old leather thing for? And why was my mouth so dry?

As the ambulance pulled around the home-run fence and across the parking lot, lights and siren going, Roger vomited into the grass behind second base. The ump called the game. Lynda's team was a church-sponsored team. Their pastor, who was also their pitcher, gathered up everyone around the pitcher's mound to pray for Lynda, and then Roger and I drove on over to the hospital to check on her.

I'm not a big God person, but I have to say the prayer helped calm and focus us. But in the car, on the way to the hospital, Roger began to whimper. It was kind of a pitiful little nasally sound, with lots of short, quick, inward breaths and lots of mucous rolling around in his sinuses. It's not a sound I ever expected Roger to make. I think maybe he was trying to hold it all together and that accounted for the weird noises. He lost it for real when we walked through the electronic doors of the ER and we got a whiff of that antiseptic odor. That's when the blubbering began in earnest. That's when he began clinging to my jersey the way my cat used to cling to our living room drapes when she was a kitten. And that's when I began having flashbacks to high school, when Roger and Lynda were an item.

I should just say this up front: I hate Roger. OK, hate may be too strong a word, but ever since he dated Lynda back in high school I've resented him. No, resent doesn't really fit either. Hatred is too strong and resentment is too mild. Somewhere in between is the word I need that describes the way I feel about Roger. So I might as well get this off my chest, since it's soggy with the snot and tears of Roger, who still clings to my wet, wrinkled jersey. I first fell in love with Lynda in junior high school. Nowadays they call it middle school, a more fitting name since you really are stuck in the middle in those years: you're half kid and half teenager, and sometimes both at once.

I sat across the aisle from Lynda in math class. She was definitely out of my league. She had boobs already, and I stared at her for most of the period.

31

In fact, I never did learn long division. Somehow I faked my way to a C in that class. She was one of the few girls with clear skin and no braces on her teeth. Also, she was somewhat aloof and had a tough reputation. There were rumors that she smoked in the restroom and that her parents didn't care how late she stayed out. She was dating a high school guy, a stocky Mexican who had served time in juvenile hall and been spotted drinking beer out behind the gym instead of going to PE class.

I guess you could say I was smitten. No, smitten sounds too cute for what I was. I was obsessed. Whatever it is in between smitten and obsessed. My brain was saturated with testosterone, my lungs weakened by asthma, and my face riddled with acne. Oh yeah, she was way out of my league. All I could do was watch her from a distance, pining in my own pitiful way as I cultivated a lifelong taste for the unobtainable.

By the time of eighth-grade commencement, my obsession had festered into a kind of sickness. Like a leper who built a comfortable shack on Father Damien's island, I learned to live with my sad fate. In the summer between junior and senior high, Lynda's Mexican disappeared after he was reputed to have killed a white guy in a gang fight, pinning the guy to the ground and grinding a corkscrew into his chest. That was the story anyway.

That same summer Roger grew about a foot and emerged from the leper colony to walk among the gods. Suddenly, he was a bull-goose jock: acne-free, dressed in all the right clothes, a top-scorer on the freshman basketball team. And just as suddenly, Lynda was crazy for him. She hung on him in the cafeteria line, draped her legs over his at the bus stop bench, kissed him with abandon right in front of the principal's office. They were the cool couple on campus — a cross between Archie and Veronica and Bonnie and Clyde, alternately winning yearbook honors as "most attractive couple" and getting suspended for skinny-dipping in the school swimming pool.

And then one day in our junior year, I walked into the drama room to retrieve my copy of Eugene O'Neill's *Ah, Wilderness!*, and there in the hallway behind the teacher's desk was Roger making out with a guy named Wayne. Wayne was a muscular kid from Oklahoma, younger by a year than us, with a crop of curly red hair that sprang from his head like a collection of thin wires. He was on the wrestling team, though not exactly a star. I had never seen two men kiss like that. It was like Clark Gable and Vivien Leigh, except not. They certainly knew what they were doing.

I dropped my book. They pulled apart. The three of us stood staring at each other. Then Wayne's face flushed and he looked at the floor. I picked up my book. Roger ran out the side door of the building, leaving Wayne alone in the hallway to shuffle his feet. Totally shocked and confused, I walked out of the drama room and all the way home, skipping Algebra.

When I walked in the front door, my mother was on the phone. "Where's your bicycle?" she asked. I shrugged. I had left it locked to the bike rack at school. She put her hand over the telephone receiver. "Are you all right?" she asked. "You look like you've seen a ghost. Why don't you bring me the thermometer?"

"I'm fine," I said, shuffling to my bedroom.

I never said a word to anyone. Not long afterwards, Roger and Lynda broke up. I'm pretty sure Wayne transferred to another school because I never saw him again. It took awhile before Roger and I could make eye contact.

Soon after graduation, Lynda got into some real trouble. She moved into an abandoned house with a bunch of squatters who were cooking methamphetamines. The sheriff's department staked out the house. The FBI sent in an undercover agent. One night when the house was filled with derelicts and dealers and cons and hookers, the SWAT team surrounded the place and hauled them all away in vans. Lynda's photo was on the front page of the *Los Angeles Times*. She was on her knees on the weedy front walkway with her hands bound behind her back and her hair down in her face. You had to look closely at the picture to see that it was her.

I once wrote a letter to her in prison, but it came back several weeks later with *This inmate has been transferred to another institution* in red ink across the bottom of the envelope. I never bothered to find out where they had moved her. All right, that's not exactly the truth. After a few beers one night I called up her mother and asked for the new address. She never even asked who I was. I think she may have been about as drunk as me. She just read the address of the prison she had been transferred to in this very flat, monotone voice. The new place was a minimum security camp up-state. I didn't even copy down the new address. The truth is by then I'd lost my nerve. When I sobered up, I tore up the letter and flushed it down the toilet. What was I thinking writing her a letter? I'm not even going to bother to recount what it said.

Lynda reappeared several years later and took a job as secretary at the United Methodist Church. Roger and I were both surprised to see her on their softball team in our Monday night co-ed league. She was just as beautiful as ever, though a little worn around the edges and several pounds heavier. When she spoke to us it was strictly baseball talk, that's all. There were rumors about her — that she'd gotten religion while in the women's penitentiary, that she'd moved back in to her parents' house after they passed away, that she lived there with a dozen cats and dogs she'd rescued from the local animal shelter. After my divorce, I took to driving past the house late at night, hatching fantasies of a "chance meeting" and mid-life romance — pitiful Lifetime channel soap opera stuff. Funny how some part of you is always stuck in junior high. Funny sad, not funny weird or funny ha-ha. The only time I saw her was on Monday evenings at the softball field. I watched her from my comfortable shack on Father Damien's island.

THE NURSE HAS just pushed open the big doors of the ER, and she's walking across the waiting room toward us. Roger's fingers tighten on my jersey. "I'm afraid I have some bad news. Your friend is in a coma," the nurse says. "We'll be transferring her soon to ICU."

"Can we see her?" I ask.

"Only family is allowed in ICU. I can give you the phone number of the nurse's station there, and you can call later to check on her condition."

"Is she going to make it?" Roger asks.

"Brain injuries are unpredictable," she says. "The first twenty-four hours are crucial. If she makes it until this time tomorrow, then her chances improve." She fishes in one of her pockets and pulls out a card, hands it to me. It's the phone number for ICU. "The trauma doctor wants to talk to you," she says. "Why don't you have a seat?"

As soon as she goes back through the big ER doors, Roger starts to cry again. He pulls himself up close to me and plants his face on my chest. Up on the silent TV screen, Bette Davis is chewing up the scenery, finally confessing to her lawyer and her husband. Her eyes are flashing the way they do when she's angling for an Oscar. I pry Roger's fingers loose. "Look," I say, "you've got to get a hold of yourself." He puts his arms around my neck. Now the other people in the waiting room are starting to stare. We're giving Bette Davis a run for her money. "Now, listen," I say, "you need to sit down."

"Noooo," he wails, in a cry that grows louder the longer he stretches out the vowel. Even the mother of the gunshot victim looks up from her *Cosmopolitan*. I grab hold of his hands, squeeze them, and push him back a little. He leans into me. I back away and wrestle free of his grip. I push him, hard, and he stumbles backward into the plastic waiting room chairs. That stops his crying. He looks at me with a look of shocked betrayal. He comes at me again, his hands outstretched, his face contorted into another crying jag. He stops when he sees me cock my fist. One more step and I'll clock him. The look on his face is the look he had back in the drama room hallway just before he bolted. But instead of running away, he sinks into a chair and buries his face into his hands.

I have an overwhelming impulse to walk away. And why not? There's no reason for me to stay here with him. He disgusts me. This is more than just resentment; it's hatred. And it's not anything between resentment and hatred; it's pure hatred. It's heady. It fills me with a kind of evil delight. I'm almost giddy with it. I can't stand to be in his presence. I never want to see him again. I could easily pick up one of these chairs right now and bring it down on his head without remorse.

He raises his head and implores me in a broken and contrite voice: "Don't leave."

The electronic doors from the parking lot slide open and in walks Lynda's pastor and two of her teammates. They go up to the nurse's window. At the opposite end of the waiting room, the big door to the ER opens and the nurse reappears. She props the door with her hip and points to us. The weary young trauma doctor tucks his clipboard under his arm and walks toward us. And though I would rather be anywhere else in the world but here, I sit down next to Roger. To my own dumbfounded surprise, I put my hand on the son of a bitch's shoulder, and I don't leave. ∎

Sisters and Brothers

IT BEGAN AS yet another rendition of the old, recurring story of jealousy and murder. Cain and Abel. Othello and Desdemona. That story. This time the setting was a college sorority, and the main characters were, as they are customarily called, sisters. They refer to themselves as big and little, the big being a year or two older and a class or two ahead of the little. In this case the little's boyfriend, a Stanford baseball player, had been seduced by her big. There was an initial confrontation in which all three parties, being drunk, behaved badly. The big sister showed no remorse for her sin. The little allowed her sense of betrayal to fill the room. For his part, the short stop boyfriend said that if he had to choose between them, and he did, he certainly did, he chose the big. The little sister stormed off.

She later tracked her big's convertible to Laguna Beach, where she and the boyfriend had retreated to plan their new life together. A second confrontation. This time the little sister produced a kitchen knife, surprising her big with a series of silent, vicious thrusts and slices. The boyfriend watched in horror. It happened so quickly, he later said. The little asked her big a few questions. The big answered in a haughty tone, relishing her conquest, gloating. Then very deliberately, the boyfriend reported, the little sister pulled the knife from her backpack; she thrust and thrust the blade as if it were a short sword. The boyfriend told the news services that he was stunned by the amount of blood that poured into the sand.

The little sister had cut two arteries and the big sister quickly bled out into the arms of the boyfriend. The news services attributed the speed of the big sister's death to the "surgical" nature of the little sister's attack, she ironically being a pre-med student. When emergency crews arrived at the beach, they noted that although the boyfriend was bathed in the girl's blood, he himself was physically unharmed. I know exactly how he felt. I wish like hell the story ended there.

TWELVE HOURS LATER I was driving north on Pacific Coast Highway, on my way to my sister's house at the crook of a small cove beneath the Santa Lucia mountains. The road is rugged and lonely along that stretch. I was surprised to see anyone, much less a lone co-ed, trudging along the road's shoulder on that foggy afternoon.

She did not have her thumb out.

Nevertheless, I pulled my pickup over into the gravel. My dog, Sonny, who had been snoozing in the backseat of the cab, yawned and stretched and sat up to see where we were. He made a little high-pitched inquisitive sound in his throat, as if to say, "Why have you stopped here?"

I watched in the driver's side mirror as she walked along, her backpack tightly strapped around an oversized Stanford sweatshirt. It was super-baggy on her and hung clear down to her thighs. The sleeves were rolled, making her look impish and cute.

The closer she got to my truck, the more excited Sonny grew. He loves any kind of company, seeing every new person as a potential Frisbee partner. She came right up to my window and said, "I don't need a ride." My Pearl Jam CD was in the stereo; I reached over and turned down the volume. I was about to ask her if she was sure, that it was a long, narrow, windy road ahead, and since we were both pointed in the same direction . . . .

But then Sonny stuck his head out the window and her whole demeanor shifted. She smiled and reached up to pet him. Sonny has that affect on people. He has one of those wide-open doggy grins, floppy ears, and goofy sad eyes that melt right through your emotional defenses. She soon discovered that a two-handed scratch behind both ears brought him to a kind of canine ecstasy, which made her forget for a moment the burden that she carried.

Sonny leapt over into the front seat as she opened the passenger door. I had to restrain him by the collar so she could climb up into the cab. He was frantically licking at her face and sniffing her sweatshirt. She stuffed her backpack with the bloody knife buried in its center down between her feet. As I pulled out onto the road I turned Pearl Jam back up. Sonny was nuzzling her sweatshirt so much it was embarrassing. Later, of course, I realized it was her blood-soaked t-shirt beneath the sweatshirt that he was after. One of the questions the reporters later asked me was if I could smell the blood on her. "I drive with the windows open," was all I could think to answer.

When Sonny began to whine and dig at her backpack, I smacked him on the butt and pushed him into the backseat. I naturally assumed she had some food for the road stuffed in there, probably with some extra clothes and maybe a few school books.

She never did buckle her seatbelt. Instead she crossed her arms and leaned back against the door. "I don't think I can keep my eyes open," she said. "Don't get any funny ideas."

"Is the music OK?" I asked.

"Fine," she said. "I like the noise. What I can't stand is silence." She leaned her head back against the window and went immediately to sleep. Sonny hung his head over the seatback and whined a little more.

"Shush," I said, pushing his muzzle back. Only later did I realize how difficult it must've been for Sonny to obey me. He must've wondered how I could be so dense as to ignore the strong, salty scent beneath that thick outer layer of cardinal-dyed cotton.

The farther north I drove, the thicker the fog.

She hadn't slept that night. Unknown to me, she had passed the hours hiding in alleys, ducking into doorways, and cautiously soliciting rides from strangers who, like me, hadn't listened to the news that evening. She slept hard. She even snored a little. I've been there, I thought, remembering how once I dozed off one night during patrols outside Ramadi, in the backseat of our Humvee, only to be jolted awake when the unit just ahead of us rolled over an IEG. Sometimes, no matter the circumstances, the body just shuts down without asking your permission.

LATER, THE REPORTERS wanted me to pretend it had been a hostage situation. "What did it feel like to be held captive in your own truck with a crazed killer who could, at any moment, use the same knife she butchered her sorority sister with against you?"

"She was just an exhausted kid," I responded. "She was no more a crazed killer than me or you." Somebody at the TV station did some research, discovered I had served two tours in Iraq, coming home with a Purple Heart. Then they wanted me to be the Heroic War Vet who bravely stood down the psycho bitch on her run from justice. "Trouble with that theory," I said directly into their camera, "is that I had no idea what she had done." And then, just to deflect them further— "She was a very sweet girl," I said. "Groggy but polite. She could've been your daughter," I said to the reporter. "For all I know, she is." That frosted him. He signaled the cameraman to shut it down, handed me his business card, and said someone from the station would be in touch to set up a more in-depth interview. "No thanks," I said, sliding the card into my mouth and chewing it like a stick of gum.

"Look, Sergeant, this story is bigger than just you, but you're an integral player. You owe it to the public to tell this part of the story. He pointed to the camera whose red light had blinked off. "They have a right to know."

I spat the wet gob that had once been his business card onto the lens of the camera.

"Have you ever fantasized about killing someone?" I asked him.

"I'm not a killer," he answered.

"But like everybody else, you've considered it."

"I fail to see the relevance," he said, gathering his notes. "You must know as well as anyone the difference between thoughts and actions."

"This is the difference right here," I said, snapping my fingers in his face. "Tell that story," I said. "Tell about how that darkness lurks in the corner of your own prim little imagination. Turn the camera on yourself. Not your smiley, dapper reporter self, but the real you."

SO LITTLE SISTER slept, chin on chest, while Sonny watched over her from the backseat, and I slowly navigated through the foggy patches along the coast highway, as Eddie Vedder growled and crooned through the speakers.

If you're at all familiar with that windy stretch of road, you know the fog comes ashore and clings to the hills and the cliffs in clumps. Sometimes it's wispy and windblown. But it can also be dense and sit for miles, with visibility down to thirty feet or so. (Try and drive at the posted speed limit then and you'll soon find yourself sailing over a cliff.)

Then all of a sudden it will break, and you'll find yourself bathed in warm sunshine, with tremendous views of the ocean for miles and miles. And then, before you know it, you enter another dark, moist patch. You touch the brakes and pray that the fool in the SUV behind you does the same. You flip on your headlights and wipers and return to squinting at the illuminated wall of gray created by your headlamps. No use the high beams—they only bounce off the fog and limit your vision even more. Fog lamps help some, but not enough to save you if a driver ahead stops or stalls.

YOU MAY BE wondering what I was doing out there on such a day. I was making my retreat from some nasty business of my own. For eight months I had been living with my girlfriend, Candace, down in La Jolla. She's an actress, Candace, and she was working on her MFA degree at UC San Diego while playing supporting roles at the Old Globe Theatre. She's no Hilary Swank, but she could hold her own on stage with just about anyone.

I was supervising a landscaping crew, not because I had any talent for it, but because I spoke a little Spanish, and the foreman on this particular job was a blood brother from our days in Iraq; we'd kept in touch through Facebook and whatnot. So when I landed in San Diego I looked him up.

One day my crew and I were regrading the soil around a new commercial complex downtown. The dozers had finished their work and been loaded back onto the flatbeds. It was all shovel work and trenchers now. My buddy the foreman got a tip from someone in INS. The big La Migra vans would be sweeping local construction sites. There's no faster way to lose a work crew. To play it safe, I paid everybody off and we quit early for the day.

When I arrived at our apartment I expected Candace to be at rehearsal. At least, I was expected to pick her up from rehearsal at the theatre later that night. So you can imagine how surprised I was to discover her there with Jules, her director from the Old Globe. He had directed her in a couple of plays, even come over to our place for dinner once or twice.

Now they were doing one of Neil Simon's comedies in which Candace had to giggle a lot. She had been practicing her giggle around the apartment for two straight weeks. It still sounded phony and overly-musical to me, but what do I know about acting? Maybe it was supposed to sound like that.

When I walked in I suddenly knew what was going on between them. My sister, when she heard, said, "Well, duh. You are so clueless when it comes to picking up crucial nuances. Frankly, I'm surprised you figured it out even then."

It's not like I walked in on them in the bedroom. But there was this heavy vibe lingering in the air of our living room. I don't know how else to say it. You know how sometimes you'll interrupt a conversation and feel there in that momentary, awkward silence that the topic of the conversation had been you—and that they weren't praising your backswing?

They were sitting on the sofa with the script open on the coffee table. There were two empty wine glasses on top of the script, and Jules' shirt was misbuttoned. They both looked flushed and guilty, talked too much and too quickly about incidentals having to do with the staging of the play. It dawned on me as I stood there listening that this wasn't a new thing but in fact a regular thing.

I retreated to the kitchen. I opened the last can of beer and stood at the kitchen sink, looking out the window at some of the neighbor kids on the play structure there on the greenbelt between apartments. The utter silence in the living room confirmed it.

When I finally walked back into the living room, they were both gone.

And here's one of those weird details that mean nothing at the time but resonate only later, upon reflection. As I was standing there at the kitchen sink, taking baby sips of the beer to make it last longer, watching the neighbor kids kick higher and higher on the swings, right there next to the sink was a wood block filled with kitchen knives.

HAVE YOU SEEN the Humphrey Bogart movie about the guy who escapes from San Quentin and goes to a mob doctor for plastic surgery to change his face? He spends half the movie hiding out in Lauren Bacall's San Francisco apartment, his head and face wrapped in bandages. He thinks that changing his face will buy him the time he needs to prove his innocence. It sounds absurd, I know, but somehow the movie makes the preposterous seem logical.

I watched that movie late one night after this whole thing had ended. And it occurred to me that ever since coming home from Iraq, I've felt like that Bogart character, wrapped up like a chrysalis. I'm not sure who I'll be when I get the bandages off, but I'm fairly certain I'm not the guy I was when I enlisted. Then again, who is?

The day after that awkward living room scene in which I slowly realized I was the third point in a ridiculous lover's triangle, as I was packing up my gear in the bedroom, Candace apologized. She said what you'd expect someone in her situation to say, that she never intended to hurt me, that she didn't know how strong her feelings for Jules were until she was past the point of no return. It was like she was talking to me on one of those kid-made phones, a string between two soup cans. I had to strain to understand her.

She said she would have ended it before the awkward living room scene, except that Jules was afraid of me. Knowing I was a vet, he thought maybe I'd go berserk and beat him to a pulp or pull a gun on him. (I don't even own any guns—gave them away when I mustered out.) She confessed she was afraid too, didn't know how my PTSD would affect me if taken by surprise. She had witnessed the headaches and the nightmares and the ear-ringing and the back pain that had recently resulted in spasms. "And you know," she said, "the emotional distance is hard to take long-term. You show more affection most days for that dog of yours than for the people in your life."

I suppose there were things I could have said back to her. As it turns out, I was ready to move on and just didn't know it. My sister has since explained to me that this is what I do. This is my deal, my "issue" as she puts it — I tune out any possible source of potential conflict or complication and move through life oblivious to the mayhem . . . to the extent that I could spend the afternoon in the company of a blood-soaked murderer and not even know it. I could slap and push my own beloved dog as he tries to warn me. For heaven's sake, I could pick up someone wandering in the middle of nowhere and not even for a moment harbor suspicion.

As I EASED around one of the hairpins on the coast highway, I saw up ahead, right next to the road, a doe and her fawn. They had followed the stream down to where it flowed beneath the roadway. On a clear day, you could see that stream as it rippled over some boulders on up the hillside, and farther down on the left you could see where it fell right down a cliffside to the ocean beneath us.

I turned off the stereo so I could hear the waterfall. It must've been the sudden absence of noise that awoke her. She had that sleepy, rub your eyes and yawn look that kids have when they come around. She stretched her arms and noticed the idyllic scene just through the windshield. It really was like one of those misty painted nature scenes the Victorians liked so much. The mother deer stood watch over her youngster as it sipped and twitched its white tail.

I pulled the truck over to the shoulder. We sat there and watched them. Sonny poked his head over the seat between us and gave out a whimper that became a mournful sort of whistle in his throat. Then the barking and the pacing began. Instead of my loyal companion, Sonny was now a caged predator who wanted nothing more than to leap from the vehicle and chase those deer as far as he could.

His barking startled the deer and sent them both into a jittery retreat beneath the roadway and through some trees. As I pulled back out onto the road and rounded the curve, Sonny stuck his head out my open window and gave them a few final sharp barks as they leapt from view.

She said, "My dad hit a deer once when we were on vacation up in Idaho. It was a dark, moonless night and the deer leapt out right in front of our RV.

43

My dad made us all stay inside while he climbed out and dragged its body by the legs over to the side of the road. I guess I was about six or seven. My brother would've been eleven or twelve. He thought it was the coolest thing ever. My mom had to physically restrain him. He wanted to pet the dead deer. My mom actually swore at him to scare him back into his seat. She never swore. My dad stood in front of the RV, lit up by the headlights, staring at the damaged bumper. He pushed and pulled and finally kicked at the bumper to try and straighten it."

"Is that where you're headed now?" I asked. "Up to see your parents?"

She turned her head away from me. "No. I don't imagine I'll see my parents again."

IN THAT BOGART movie, there's a scene where Bacall removes the bandages from Bogie's face, peeling away the gauze to reveal his new features. He looks at himself in the mirror, rubs his whiskers the way he does in all his movies. He seems happy with the mob surgeon's handiwork. He showers and shaves and puts on a clean shirt.

When he comes downstairs, Bacall's got his favorite record playing on the hi-fi, a cool bebop jazz number, and she's cooked him dinner. They drink a toast. You can just about smell the steaks cooking and taste the martini as it passes over your tongue and slides down your throat. The view through Bacall's window shows the post-war San Francisco skyline all lit up. Neither one of them says so, but they're in love, just like in all their movies, just as they apparently were in real life.

But the movie's only half over at that point, and you know the world outside Bacall's stylish apartment is not going to open its arms and embrace them. Outside there's blackmail and murder and sour romance, the usual stuff you see in those movies, the stuff that stands in the way of true love and tranquility.

THE PAIN IN my back was coming on again. I adjusted my pillow and cracked open a can of beer. I washed down a Vicodin. That's one thing the VA has no end of — Vicodin. They'll give you enough to last through the next war, and maybe the one after that.

"Want a beer?" I asked, pointing to the six-pack on the seat between us.

"Sure." She pried a can free of the plastic rings. "Where is it you're going?" she asked.

"My sister has a place up ahead. Her husband's a big-time real estate lawyer in Santa Barbara. They own this huge house, but it's old and it's falling apart down around their ears." She drained her beer like it was water. "Have another," I said. "Anyway she's invited me up to do some renovations. The roof needs tar and shingles. The plumbing moans and groans. She wants me to strip off the old wallpaper and paint it. Bring the house up into the new century."

"You don't talk like a construction guy."

"I went to college once, too."

She got herself another can and cracked it open. Sonny stuck his head up next to hers.

"Sonny," I said, sharply pulling at his collar. "Sorry. Sometimes I give him a sip. He thinks he can mooch from anyone."

"Does he drink from the can?" she asked.

"You can pour some into his bowl." I pointed to it on the floor next to her backpack. "But don't feel obligated."

She poured Sonny a drink and he lapped it up. She laughed as he licked her face with his beery tongue.

"But the real reason my sister invited me up is so she can put my life in order. She believes, given time, that she can fix me."

"Fix you? Are you broken?"

"No more than anyone else," I said. "But she's got a plan for me that sounds better than any I've made for myself. Oh, you can just toss the empties into the backseat. Sonny'll lick them clean and I'll drop them in the recycle bin later."

"What's the plan?" she asked.

"The plan involves less beer and Vicodin and more 'good hard work,' as she puts it. The plan involves church on Sundays, babysitting my nephews, finding a good woman who's not an actress, and sending down roots in the community. By roots I take it she means staying in one place for awhile. Stability, she says, is the key component of the plan."

"Well," she said. "That is surely a plan." She looked directly at me. "And I wish you sincere and supreme luck with it."

"And what about you?" I asked.

"My plan sort of blew up in my face. But I should have stuck to it anyway."

"I take it you're a Stanford scholar."

She tugged at her sweatshirt a little. "My boyfriend is. Was. Still is, I guess. My ex-boyfriend." She said it in such a way that even I knew not to inquire further.

THE FOG THINNED to wispy strips as we approached the little village just ten miles south of my sister's place. I suppose village is a generous name for it. There's a gas station, an art gallery/antique shop, and a mom and pop general store. As I pulled up to the little store, the sun shone brightly overhead, even though the woods all around were shrouded in the deep, gray, drippy fog. Here and there you could see rays of sunlight breaking through.

"Want anything?" I asked.

"No, thanks," she answered, "I'm beyond wanting."

"I'll be right back," I said. I grabbed Sonny's bowl and took him around to the side of the building where there's a water faucet. I filled his bowl and went inside.

The lady who owns the place greeted me as I came through the screen door. It's a place that might go back to the days of Bogart and Bacall, a wooden shack with a couple of old-time gas pumps out in the weeds that haven't worked for decades. They sell sodas and snacks to travelers and milk and bread to the locals.

When I came out of the restroom, I grabbed another six-pack from the cold cabinet and a Slim Jim and a pack of chewing gum. I tossed two bags of Skittles on the counter for my nephews. As I was paying, the lady behind the counter said, "Looks like your girl took off."

"What's that?"

"The girl in your truck. She ran into the trees while you were in the restroom."

The passenger door of the truck stood open. Sonny was gone. I took the path through the woods just beyond the old gas pumps. I whistled for Sonny and heard him bark up ahead. That bark was an answer to my whistle, but the series of more urgent barks that followed was a reaction to something that had happened ahead on the trail.

The fog was thick in there, hung like heavy wool in the trees. You could see the tree trunks and the ferns. You could smell that salty brine that hangs in the coastal air at low tide. And you could hear waves crashing against rocks in the distance. I held my arms out in front of me like you do in a dark, unfamiliar house. As long as Sonny kept barking I kept walking. When he stopped I stopped. When he started up again I moved forward. I called out to him. I would've called the girl's name had I known it. I followed Sonny's bark, louder and closer.

There's no railing along the edge of the cliff there. If you were walking at a good clip you could possibly slip over the edge. The police who examined all three of our footprints explained that mine were shuffling and cautious, hers were confident and deliberate, showed no sign of hesitation, and Sonny's circled the girl's prints, as if he were trying to slow her down, get in her way. According to the investigators, the girl picked up her pace with each step and fairly flew over the edge.

Sonny stood at that edge and barked once more when I finally arrived, as if to say, "What took you so long?" Then he fell silent. Standing next to him, I could hear the waves hitting the rocks below. The fog was blowing across the face of the cliff. As it did, the ocean became visible, then disappeared again.

She had clipped her heavy backpack tightly to her torso, which is why it took a couple days to recover her body. She got banged up quite a bit on the rocks and went out with the swift tide. She eventually got tangled in a kelp forest about half a mile from shore. The Coast Guard divers had a hell of a time cutting her loose.

THE BOGART MOVIE ends with him nursing a drink at a cafe table somewhere in a friendly fictional South American locale, a ragtag samba band playing on the bandstand, an ocean vista on the painted backdrop. He's escaped his trouble back in the states, but at great cost. He's all alone now.

Bacall walks in. She quietly instructs the band leader to play their tune, the cool jazzy one that accompanied their dinner the night she removed the bandages from his fresh layer of facial skin. When he hears the first few notes, he looks up from his drink, as if someone has just addressed him in his mother tongue after long immersion in a foreign language. His eyes scan the room.

She crosses the crowded dance floor. She had that way of walking, you know, the way she walked in all their movies, with a certain slinky confidence, probably because they were in love in real life, and she could bring some of their private signals into their movie life. They had this famous thing together — the older guy on his second or third go around, with a reputation to live down, and the teenaged theatre usherette turned fashion model turned movie star, who was fresh but also sophisticated in her tall, thin, elegant way. And her walk across the crowded room towards him had become a kind of hallmark for her, a silent monologue of the body.

No matter what kind of trouble had preceded this moment, the future was all peace and prosperity. The war was behind them. The violence of the San Francisco underworld was hundreds of miles away. It was a kind of Latin Eden they had discovered as the music rose and the credits rolled.

YOU MAY HAVE seen me interviewed on the TV news that night. It wasn't much to see. I was a disappointment to the reporter because I knew nothing then about her crime. "She was exhausted," I said, "and maybe a bit sad, but who isn't?"

He signaled the camera operator to turn away from me. He proceeded to do what they all do, I guess, spin the story the way they're trained. And so in his terms, the girl in the baggy Stanford sweatshirt who liked my dog and shared a couple beers with me became the psycho sorority killer, and I who had narrowly escaped becoming her next victim was clearly suffering from shock.

Then they cut to footage of her big sister and all the good she had accomplished in her short life and all the people she had touched with her volunteer work. You've heard it many times before if you've paid any attention to the news at all. This was the same reporter who's business card I spat out when he tried to interview me the next day, and the day after that, until another sexier tragedy occurred and the news crews picked up and moved on.

I've thought a lot about all three of them these past couple weeks. The girl in the Stanford sweatshirt. The girl she killed. I've also considered her boyfriend, who was depicted as a coward by the media because he hadn't stepped between the big sister and her knife-wielding little. I myself have killed sixteen men that I know of, which is to say I inflicted mortal wounds on the bodies of sixteen enemy combatants. And I've fought next to five of my own blood brothers as they died, most of them swiftly but one of them slowly and in my arms.

I carry them all with me, day by day, as I trudge up the ladder with hammer and nails. Lug them on my back as I crawl beneath my sister's house with a flashlight and a wrench. Schlep them to the dinner table, to church on Sundays, and up the stairs at night to my attic bedroom, where I watch old movies and sip my secret stash of beer. I'm sticking to the plan as much as possible. If you find a better way, let me know. If you've figured out how to reach that little cafe table with the ocean view and the love of your life moving towards you to the tune of your favorite song, the violence and the sadness all behind you, please, for the love of God, let me know. ∎

Who Could Hang a Name on You?

APRIL 16, 10:15 P.M. A dark sedan hit its brakes, idled like a growling beast for a moment, then quickly turned into the church parking lot, its tires squealing. Shouts pierced the quiet spring evening. The headlights came straight at the old man, who was sitting in the front seat of his dilapidated Toyota, feeding his cat on the dashboard from a yogurt container. The car screeched to a stop a few feet from the old man's Toyota, but the headlights did not go off. Loud yelps emerged from the car and the boom-boom of the bass on the car's radio filled the old man's ears. Another light, brighter than the headlights, now shone on the old man. The cat arched her back and jumped into the stack of freshly-laundered clothes in the backseat.

The doors of the car sprung open and four jubilant young men hopped out, shouting obscenities. One of them held a spotlight. Another balanced a video camera, which was pointed at the old man. One had a tennis racket. And the one who climbed out of the driver's seat held a baseball bat in one hand. "You fucking piece of shit," he yelled. "You waste of human flesh." He cocked the bat and quickly smashed it into the windshield. The glass shattered into a large spider web pattern. The old man held his hands up over his face while the young man continued to swing at the windshield, eventually punching out most of the glass. Glancing toward the light, the old man could see that the one with the video camera was filming this.

The young man with the tennis racket pulled the old man's car door open, grabbed him by the arm, and yanked him out. The old man crouched against the car, tucking his head under his arms, as the young man beat him with the racket. The one with the baseball bat continued to smash up the old man's Toyota, stopping now and then to take a threatening swing at the old man. Exposed by his sleeveless t-shirt, his thick biceps were both encircled by thorny tattooed wreaths. One of the young men pulled out a knife and slashed the old man's tires. The loud music from the car served as their soundtrack. "Are you getting this?" the one with the baseball bat and the thorny tattoos shouted to the one with the camera. The one with the tennis racket began to rip the upholstery and tear apart the Toyota's overhead lining.

BACK: THAT MORNING. 7:35 A.M. The old man awoke to the sound of an approaching siren. The parking brake was lodged up against his tailbone again and the cat, as always, lay curled on his chest. When the siren drew closer, she stood on her three legs and stretched, kneading the old man's sweater with her front claws. Then the cat yawned and stretched her rear leg out behind her. He scratched her neck, and she lifted her head to receive the pleasure of his long nails up under her chin. The old man turned and massaged his tailbone, adjusting so that he could also pull himself into a seated position. He grabbed hold of the steering wheel for balance and accidentally leaned on the horn, which frightened the cat and sent her into the backseat. There she sank into his pile of dirty clothes.

He turned himself to face the windshield and maneuvered his feet to the floor, catching a glance at his reflection in the rear view mirror. "There he is again," he said aloud, "Quasimodo arises." He flipped the mirror up. The siren blared louder and louder. "The bells of Notre Dame," he said to the cat. Across the church parking lot, he could see the young pastor's car, a beat up Volkswagen Jetta, parked next to the church office. The pastor didn't mind if the old man parked there overnight, but he needed him to move the car during normal business hours. A few of the elderly ladies in the congregation, who met for their weekly quilting club in Fellowship Hall, were frightened by his presence and offended by the astringent odor. The sun had already hit the peak of the church's roof and begun to climb the steeple, toward the cross. The siren passed one block to the east and its wail receded into the distance. "You know what that siren means, cat? That means that somebody's morning is going worse than ours. There's something to be said for that."

When he opened the driver's side door, the cat bounded to the asphalt and made a beeline for the spindly trees that lined the edge of the church parking lot. Scuffing along in his flip-flops, he followed the cat and emptied his bladder there against the cement cinder block wall that separated the church parking lot from the houses in the surrounding neighborhood. Beyond the wall, mothers roused sleepy children and called them to breakfast, father's warmed up cars in driveways and sipped the dregs of the coffee while checking the baseball standings, dogs barked at birds on the dew-drenched lawns. Or so he remembered from growing up in such a neighborhood, with its suburban morning routines. Way back when.

The cat climbed up a volunteer privet shoot and leapt atop the cement wall. She was off to find her breakfast and to fend as best she could for herself, taking leftovers from the neighborhood pets and nabbing the occasional scrub jay. The cat looked back at him. The old man saluted. "Happy pickings," he said.

Forth: 10:21 p.m. The old man lay on the ground now, watching, as the young man with the camera moved in and around the vehicle, filming the damage and filming the old man as he cowered. They tossed the clean clothes from the Toyota's backseat out on the dirty asphalt. "Fuck yeah!" the one with the baseball bat yelled. He twirled the bat around in one hand like a baton, making his thorny tattoo ripple. The old man felt something warm splashing against his head. There was general laughter now among all four of the young men, punctuated by the occasional yelp. He thought he recognized the laughter. Were these the ones who had heckled and harassed him in the coffee shop earlier? He turned his head and realized the one holding the spotlight was pissing on him. The one with the camera came around to get a close-up of the old man's face. The one with the baseball bat held the old man's hair so the camera could get a clear shot of the piss splashing onto the open cuts on the old man's face.

"You need a shower, meat," the one with the baseball bat said. "You fucking stink." He craned the old man's neck so his mouth opened. "Marinate the meat," he said.

The one holding the camera could hardly contain himself as he shook with laughter.

"Hold the fucking camera still," the one with the bat said.

The one with the spotlight finished pissing.

"Here," the one with the bat said to the one with the camera, "wait a minute, press pause for a sec." The young man with the baseball bat returned to the car and traded the bat for a golf club. "Now, get this," he said. "Press the fucking record button and get this."

The old man saw what was coming and he turned away from the one who cocked the golf club up over his head. He covered the back of his head with his hands. His second grade teacher had taught him to do this in school in case the Soviet Union launched a nuclear attack against the U. S. It was called a "duck and cover" drill, and it had finally come in handy.

Oddly, neither the bat nor the golf club hurt nearly as much as the tennis racket. The golf club merely bounced off the old man's back and shoulders, but the racket stung like a giant wasp. The young man with the golf club was growing tired now, from swinging so hard, but his adrenaline was high enough that he found it difficult to stop hitting the old man. Something in his brain was getting a real charge. Some sort of ancient fuel kept him swinging, even as the club glanced off the old man again and yet again. "Fuck yeah!" the young man shouted.

BACK: 9:45 A.M. He stopped in at the YMCA for his morning shower and free donuts and coffee. Then he drove over to the community college with two large plastic trash bags tucked into his belt. The recycle bins were overflowing with empty soda cans, water bottles, and energy blends. He lifted the wooden lids, slipped on his latex gloves, and started in. He plucked out the cans and bottles, tucking them into his plastic bags. As he walked from bin to bin, he looked at the students, who seemed not to notice him. He was used to it. He was the Invisible Man. As a kid, he had loved the famous Claude Rains movie. At certain times in his youth, he had imagined injecting himself with the mysterious serum, unraveling his bandages, and disappearing into the world like a phantom.

Not much studying went on at the community college as far as he could see. If their overheard conversations were to be believed, the students were mostly concerned about not getting arrested for the petty larcenies they committed against each other and their employers. He thought that if he had the chance to go back to school, he wouldn't waste the opportunity, like these kids seemed to be doing. Then again, school wasn't really his thing. He had been happier in the army. Looking back, he wished he had stayed in the army. He had volunteered for covert operations during the Vietnam War and served out most of his time at a remote listening post in the mountains of Laos. The boys he had gone through boot camp with had ended up in the thick of it—hellish jungle combat, the tunnels, the snipers, the boredom, the drudgery, the endless coming and going of the choppers, and the body bags. Maybe if he had stuck with it and reenlisted he would've learned to cope with the lack of personal freedom. But he was still young then, and he thought what he wanted was to wake up every morning without a plan and without obligations.

FORTH: 10:32 P.M. His face to the asphalt, the camera rolling, the lights bearing down on him, the boom-boom of the car radio pounding, the tennis racket now joining in on the fun, the old man began to think what an odd and strangely familiar thing this was that was happening. It had happened so often, the old man thought, in the history of the human race. Here were four young men, teeming with hormones and vigor, who had found someone they could exercise their hatred upon. He had thought about this quite a bit back when he was in the army. The sergeants had trained them through numerous drills to turn this sort of hatred on and off, to use it under orders and then just shut off the switch, take a shower, and go on over to the mess hall.

The old man put his hands over his ears to block the tumult. He struggled to follow a clear line of thought. He began to wonder, though, about those who would watch the video for entertainment, probably later tonight, on some web site or other. They would sit in the comfort of their homes and watch some old homeless guy being beaten and pissed on and abused, and then maybe they would check their email and the baseball scores, before brushing their teeth and heading off to bed. He remembered somebody telling him a story a while back about snuff videos on the Internet. Suddenly the old man realized that the goal here might just be to beat him to death.

BACK: 3:30 P.M. Except for the old man, the laundromat was empty. He liked it that way. Mornings and evenings were too crowded, and the competition for dryers made him anxious. But afternoons there was only the soothing sound of the machines with their metallic wobbling and the mild chugging of their overworked motors. He had washed his three loads in the front washers — all the clothing he had, save the jeans and Sticky Fingers t-shirt he now wore — and sat waiting for the dryers to finish their cycle. As they spun, he sat in the molded plastic chairs and flipped through an old issue of *People* magazine. Another television star had gone into rehab after driving her Alfa Romeo into the ocean at Malibu. Another politician had slept with another intern and made her pregnant and his wife furious. Another aging rock star had failed to recapture his fan base in an attempted come-back tour. But wait a minute. This time he recognized the aging rock star. It was Carl, the front man for Electric Zinnia, the band the old man had played guitar in for eighteen months.

After his stint in the army, he had taken up guitar for a while and gotten good enough to play with a band of hippies he met on a commune in Alabama. He was older than the other guys in the band, already thirty in fact. He liked them because they weren't sure where they fit in either, and they didn't ask too many questions or form snap judgments. He and the band had hitchhiked together across the country, playing music in coffee shops and nightclubs, spending all the money the army had paid him when he mustered out. Once in LA, they had somehow gotten the interest of an agent, who booked them as one of many opening acts at the Whiskey-a-Go-Go on the Sunset Strip.

And here was Carl, looking up at him from the pages of *People* magazine, caught by the paparazzi emerging from a cheap motel room in Houston with an under-aged girl he swore was his niece. The band had broken up for some reason. What was it? He couldn't remember now, an argument over a booking or a prospective record deal or a girl. Carl had put out two hit solo records in the years following. That was, what, forty years ago now? And here was Carl, looking up at him from the tattered pages of *People*.

A young Asian woman entered the laundromat with a basket of clothes under one arm. Her opposite hand held a cell phone to one ear. "Check it out," the old man said, holding up the magazine. "It's Carl. It's my pal, Carl." He stood a little too abruptly to show her the photo. He may have stumbled toward her awkwardly. Startled, she backed away, saying, "Please, no." She dropped her cell into the laundry and fumbled in her purse, pulling out a small spray can, which she pointed at the old man. She backed out the door and scurried around the corner. The old man gathered up his laundry and beat it. He never knew when someone was going to call the cops on him. He prided himself on staying out of trouble. He was the Invisible Man, and he wanted to keep it that way.

FORTH: 10:35 P.M. "Stop!" the old man heard someone shout. "Stop this now!" The loud music snapped off. "Back away from him!" he heard a voice say. The beating had stopped. The old man turned to see the young pastor from the church standing between him and the other young men. The spotlight switched off.

"Who the fuck are you, dickwad?" the one with the golf club said. "You want some of this, too?"

"I called the cops," the pastor said.

"You what?" The young man cocked the golf club. The pastor raised his arms to block it. The young man swung hard. The old man could hear the ulna bone break. It was the same sound, more or less, as a long drive off the tee.

The pastor cried out in pain. He dropped to his knees, holding his arm. The young man with the tennis racket brought it hard across the pastor's face, turning his head. "You asked for this, bitch," said the one who held the spotlight at his side. He raised the spotlight up over the pastor's head. The old man found himself standing. Without really thinking about it, he reached up and grabbed the hand that held the spotlight. They stood locked together momentarily, as if striking a pose, and then the golf club came down across the old man's back, and the tennis racket whipped him right in the face, knocking him flat again.

There was a moment of silence, and then they heard a siren approaching.

The young men all tossed their sports and video equipment into their car, jumped inside, slamming the doors, while the one with the thorny biceps who had swung the baseball bat and the golf club with such joyful precision drove the car straight backwards until they were out of the lot and back on the road. The car radio was switched back on. The one with the camera leaned out of his window and filmed the wreckage as they drove away. The loud boom-boom of the bass receded into the night.

BACK: 8:20 P.M. The old man stood on the walkway above the cliffs and watched the waves come in. He watched the people walking their dogs on the sand below. He watched the kids on their skateboards doing 360s, the moms with their strollers, the teenagers holding hands. Carl's photo in *People* had made him feel agitated. Sure, it brought back a few nice memories of those days, but mostly it made him hyper-aware that forty years had passed him by in a wink. Other people — those passing him on their evening constitutionals, for instance — had led real lives during those years. Once he had been a lanky kid with a cool Fender guitar paid for by the US Army, prancing about the stage, playing the part of the hippie rock star. And then somehow God had hit the pause button on his life. Or had he himself done that? Now he was a bum. There was no other word for it. He often overheard it whispered by parents grabbing their children's hands while he walked by. A devil wind of decades had whirled around him, leaving him standing more or less in the same spot. He had kept his distance from everyone, minded his own business, worked just enough in gas stations and copier shops, on landscaping teams and paint crews to keep himself free of the shelters and, for the most part, out of jail.

But it had been a long time since he'd had a room of his own. Did he even have any relatives left? He had stood here on the walkway overlooking the beach, a few blocks from Huntington Beach pier, staring out to sea, watching other people rush by on bicycles, on foot, with cell phones to their ears and day planners in their fanny packs. He was missing something that most everyone else seemed to have: they all spent their days cultivating and maintaining relationships—with family members, employers, friends, pets. People had come and gone in his life, but rarely had they made much of a difference to him. Like the nameless cat that shared his car at night, they each fulfilled a small need with no further connection. Well, if there was something missing in him, it was far too late in the game to acquire it now.

After weighing his bags of cans and bottles on the scales at the recycle center and pocketing his money, he walked down and got in line for his evening cup of joe. The sun was dropping quickly into the ocean and the moon already shone overhead. The sky was pink and orange out over Catalina Island; it was a deep, rich blue directly above.

The teenagers were out in force. It must be Friday night, the old man thought. Friday night was the night when all the kids in town were rowdiest. Enslaved by school and family obligations during the week, they behaved like animals released from the zoo on Friday night. He vaguely remembered feeling that way himself once. Friday night and a full moon. The hospitals, jails, and madhouses would be screaming busy tonight. All the old man wanted now was a large cup of coffee to sip in the corner of the shop by the window. He could see the moon from there. He could watch the night come on, and he could stay out of everybody's way.

Forth: 10:38 p.m. The old man had never heard a man weep in agony as the young pastor was now. He was rocking as he clutched his broken arm, the bone bulging against his skin. A siren wailed out on the boulevard. The old man struggled to stand and made his way over to his old Toyota; it was completely thrashed, inside and out. He rummaged around a bit in what had been the back seat. He stood straight up and stretched his arms and legs, wincing at the sharp pains that stabbed at every joint. He found the moon shining through the branches of the privet tree right next to the car. Ah, there she was, the three-legged cat, balanced on a lower branch. He reached up and grabbed hold. He checked her over.

She seemed all right. He put her on the ground and walked back to check on the pastor. There was vomit all down the front of his clerical shirt. He was breathing heavily through his mouth.

BACK: 8:45 P.M. A group of teenage boys came up behind him in line at the coffee shop; they began to mock him. One of the boys held his nose and made sure everyone saw that he was offended by the old man's body odor. It was a funny bit, and it got the kid some laughs from his friends, which pumped him up a bit. So he began to taunt the old man. "Hey, grizzly, you like coffee? You having your first cup after winter hibernation? Hey, dude, which cave did you crawl out of?"

He and his friends laughed at their own cleverness. The old man thought it was pretty clever, too. He could not begrudge them a little fun, even at his own expense. He turned and made a face like a grizzly bear and held up his hands like claws. At first, they backed nervously away from him, but then they broke out in loud chuckles and guffaws. "Whoa," said the boy, "that is some freaky bear face. Dude, you scared us. You really are a bear, aren't you? Do that again." They continued laughing. "Hey, do that again," he said.

One of his buddies said, "Dude, don't feed the bears." This sent them into uncontrollable peals of laughter. The first boy poked the old man from behind. "Careful," said his friend, "you never know when a bear in the wild might turn on you."

The first boy poked at the old man again, harder this time. "That true, grizzly bear? You gonna turn on me, dude? Is Smokey gonna go wacko on us?"

The old man turned and looked the boy in the eyes. Often this was enough to stop this sort of thing. It had worked before.

"That's enough, you guys," the employee in the green apron behind the counter said. He brought the old man his large cup of coffee and took his money. The old man picked up his cup and began to walk toward the corner. But before his third step, his left foot was kicked out from under him; he tripped and fell flat on the tile floor. His coffee spilled everywhere. The old man sat up, somewhat dazed, looking around him. The boys were laughing uproariously now. "I said that's enough!" he heard the man behind the counter say. "Out!"

"What?" the boys protested. The first boy said, "We didn't do anything. I can't help it if the grizzly bear can't walk. He's probably drunk. Hey, you wasted, old bear? Is Baloo hung over?"

"Out!" the man insisted.

The boys turned to go. The first boy made the scary bear face at the old man on his way out the door as they continued on, leaving a wake of giggles and chortles. The man wearing the green apron came around the counter with a mop. He helped the old man to his feet and brought him another cup of coffee. The other people in the coffee shop pretended not to notice what had happened. He would have to find another coffee shop now, one where nobody would recognize him as the goofy grizzly sprawled on the tile floor, unwilling or unable to defend himself.

FORTH: 10:40 P.M.   Red and blue lights flashing, a cop car wheeled into the lot, tires squealing, the white spotlight pointed right at him. Déjà vu. The cruiser pulled up to the spot where the other car had been only moments ago. The siren stopped. The voice over the cruiser's loudspeaker said, "Freeze. Stay right were you are, motherfucker."

The old man smiled for the first time in a long time. It was the funniest thing he could remember hearing. The red and blue lights continued to sweep around and around the parking lot, making him feel woozy and weak in the knees. He sat right down and began to chuckle lightly to himself. He could stay right where he was, you bet. No problem. But the chuckle produced a cough, and the coughing encouraged him to spit up what looked like a gob of blood and mucous onto the asphalt. Yes, he would stay right where he was. That was something he knew well how to do. He heard the cops on their radio asking for paramedics. One of the cops had his gun drawn and pointed at the old man from behind his open car door. It would take some time to sort this out.

He looked over at his beat up Toyota, at the glass and upholstery and clothing that littered the asphalt around them. He looked at the pastor cradling his broken arm, at the cat now purring and rubbing against his leg. They were sprawled on the pavement like the survivors of a bad wreck. The old man looked into the battered and bleeding face of the young pastor. He looked like a rookie prize-fighter who'd gone six rounds against the champ. The pastor had sacrificed his own safety for him, and the old man had somehow reciprocated. He thought he should say something. "What's your name?" he asked.

The pastor formed the word with difficulty, "Ben."

"My mother called me Gabriel," the old man replied. "You can call me Gabe."

The pastor nodded. Another siren approached. No, two more sirens, coming from different directions.

The old man looked over at the cops. One was talking into his shoulder radio. The other still had his gun poised on the two men. "If we live through this," he said, "we'll sleep on clean sheets tonight. Amen?"

He reached across and wiped some of the blood from the pastor's nose onto his own hand. He held up his bloody palm and showed it to the cops. The cop who had been talking on his radio turned his attention to his partner. The old man couldn't hear what he said to the other cop because the sirens now began to drown out all other sound. As in a silent movie, the music of the siren played over the pantomimed exchange between the cops. Finally, the one with the gun stood erect and holstered his weapon. The cat rubbed herself along the length of the old man's thigh, and then she curled into his lap. ▪

Equipoise

THE FIRST TIME was a complete accident. I awoke with a ringing in my ears. I lay on a public walkway without any idea of how I had come to be there. I had a memory of feeling light-headed, then outright dizzy. I had put my arms out and looked towards my wife. Had I asked her for help?

An oily substance filled the corner of my eye and I became aware of pain — sharp pain — right in the center of my forehead. I reached up and fingered the edges of an open cut between my eyebrows. As I looked down at my fingers, I could see the sticky red substance, but I could not name it. What was this stuff? I had seen it somewhere before.

All right. I had fallen. That much seemed clear. I had split open my forehead. That, too, slowly became evident. My wife was speaking into a small device in her hand. This was blood I was rubbing between my fingers. My blood. And it was me my wife was talking about when she said into the device that I had been unconscious but was now awake. It was our location she was trying to describe on her . . . what was that thing called? A cell phone.

She put her hand on my chest and spoke directly to me now. "The paramedics are on their way," she said.

"I'm sorry," I said. I'm not sure why I said that. I had the feeling that I had caused her some trouble and that our afternoon was about to take a different direction from what we had planned. What was it we had planned? Where were we walking to when I suddenly blacked out and fell to the pavement on my face?

It was three days later when I was discharged from the hospital. They had stitched up my forehead first in the ER, then run a CAT scan to see if there was any blood on the brain. There wasn't. I had a mild concussion. They drew a lot of blood. The neurologist interviewed me, then ordered an MRI and an EEG. For those three days they monitored my heart and my blood pressure. They ran every test they could think of that might reveal what had toppled me. In the end, the neurologist called it a vasovagal episode. My primary care doctor guessed it was a reaction to my blood pressure medication, which contained niacin, an organic compound that causes intense flushing in high doses.

I must confess I rather enjoyed it. To be the center of a puzzle that must be solved — that is a very satisfying position for a frail human ego. To be under the microscope, so to speak, of several bright minds, transforms you into a minor celebrity while it lasts. After my discharge from the hospital, I began to miss the attention.

The second time was also accidental. Or was it? I was looking skyward at a plane whose engines had sputtered when I tripped on the wheel of a stroller and dropped to the sidewalk. I never lost consciousness. I did not bleed. But, oh, the bruises and the aches that followed!

A small crowd of people came to my aid. They cooed, lifted me to my feet, brushed the leaves from my jacket. Was I OK, was I hurt bad, did I need a ride anywhere, could they call someone for me?

No, no, fine, thank you. Ow, well it hurts a little. But I'm OK, thanks.

Well, take it easy now, watch your step, keep your eyes on the path.

Right. Thanks, thanks.

The rest of the day I was puffed up by their attention. I began to watch the sky more attentively. I found myself scuffing instead of marching. Would it be so bad if I fell again? There was something vaguely spiritual about it. Seeing someone take a spill brings out the best in people, allows them to show a little tenderness. To be the agent of such compassion — it could be a kind of calling. And the physical sensation began to appeal to me. Falling was sweet surrender.

This all came on rather suddenly. There is only one possible antecedent. As a child I remember enjoying scabs, especially on my knees and elbows. The way the brown and crusty patches grew then receded fascinated me. I was not much for picking at them, but rubbing, yes, I would rub the bumpy surface of those lovely scabs until they began to crumble around the edges, revealing the tender reddish new skin beneath.

The third time I planned it all; worse, I had begun to think of it as an art form. I found a minor staircase near a crowd of populated cafe tables in the center of the zoo. I was a stone's throw from the shallow pink flamingo pond and adjacent to the avenue of small Asian monkeys in large cages. It went well, I thought. I made a small noise at the top of the steps, the kind of sucking noise you might emit if you turned your ankle. I reached for the steel railing with one hand to soften the initial fall. Then down the first few steps I went with a twist and a turn, landing on my left hip and rolling my way down the remaining steps, ass over tea kettle. I took care not to involve my head in any way.

The stitches had just been removed and I wore a marvelous red scar right down the middle of my forehead.

I was not perfectly all right, however. In fact, that left hip of mine retained a deep bruise — enough so that I needed a cane for many weeks afterwards.

When I hit bottom I lay there stunned. The wind had been knocked out of me. I really did need the help that soon arrived. People leapt from their cafe tables. They told me not to get up. They checked my pupils. Someone retrieved my glasses, which were slightly bent out of shape, from the concrete. I refused the ambulance. Instead, the zoo sent its own nurse to my side. She loaded me into her little golf cart and took me to her little medical hut behind the gift shop. She checked my blood pressure, asked what medication I was on, suggested I call my primary care physician. She made a brief phone call to the zoo's lawyer before sending me on my way. All in all, it was a marvelous afternoon. I've certainly never enjoyed a trip to the zoo as much before or since.

For my next fall I wanted to be airborne. As the heroin user tries snorting before the needle, I wanted to experience the rush of flight while minimizing the physical damage. I was no Evel Knievel, but I was on the lookout for my next stunt.

One day I was walking a friend's dog in the park and came to an old stone bridge that arched over a lower path. At mid-span, the drop was about eight feet. Too far and too obvious. But the image of falling over the edge and *rolling* toward the lower path seemed an attractive alternative. I let go of the dog's leash and stepped up onto the stacked-stone wall that lined the bridge and leapt — I suppose that's the word for it — down onto the grassy slope.

The drop was farther than I had calculated and I hit the ground hard, rolling downward out of control. The initial jolt was a great shock to the joints and every glorious bump, mogul, and rock along the way added more pain and more thrill to the ride.

Before I knew it, I was on my back on the path directly beneath the bridge. The dog barked at me from its peak. The tall trees were thinning of their yellow and orange leaves, and I lay there looking at the gray clouds above them. The pain in my neck and back quickly began to subside. It was here, on my back, gazing up at the sky, that I took note of the naturalness of the prone position, of the way the soft, moist soil of the earth had received me. Think of it: our struggles in this life all stem from our stubborn attempts to stand upright. Lie on your back and feel in your bones the earth move beneath you and the sky spin its cloudy magic overhead.

Into this reverie soon broke other dog-walkers and joggers who came upon me with the usual concerned utterances. Their compassion held little interest for me now. In fact, I no longer needed an audience. The do-gooders helped me to my feet, reunited me with my friend's dog, and parted with the usual take-it-easy-nows and you-be-carefuls. People are so good that way. We love to send each other on our way with good wishes.

I understood now that I could not continue to nurture this vocation. It would only lead to a flight from the fourth floor balcony and a hard landing on top of the taxi cab parked at the curb below. As it turns out, my elbow swelled that afternoon and my ankle began to throb. I relished the discomfort the rest of the day, resisting the ice pack and the Ibuprofen.

I began to dream of the next excursion, the finale to my short-lived addiction. Everywhere I went I pictured myself tumbling uncontrollably — tipping from the top of a step ladder, launching down into an open manhole, rolling from the backseat of a moving car. For my final performance I needed something dangerous but not obviously suicidal. There was no longer any need for an audience. I wanted to be scared, but I wanted to walk away. No ambulances.

Walking home from work one afternoon I came upon a large maple tree — just the ticket. I set my briefcase at the base of the trunk. It had low branches, easy to mount, but they were just far enough apart to present a challenge. Attracting no attention whatsoever, I slowly and, if I may say so myself, elegantly, climbed the tree. It was the work of a bipedal primate whose distant ancestors may have swung from such trees. I did it with the ease of certain eastern European circus acrobats.

The upper branches were thin as my arm and swayed under my weight. I enjoyed the view momentarily. Then I began to bounce upon one of the narrow branches. It didn't take long for it to snap, beginning my quick descent. I hit several branches on the way down as my body turned and bounced from branch to branch. If someone were beneath the tree at the time they might've thought there were a family of rambunctious apes overhead. It was just me up there, though not for long.

There was nothing elegant about the fall. I had been flipped into the head down position. As soon as I realized this, I reached out and hooked a branch, halting my momentum. The stable branch gave me the fulcrum to turn around, while nearly dislocating my right shoulder. My feet dangled momentarily, and then I dropped to the ground below. As I think back on it now, I hear in my mind a crashing sound. That was me, of course. That was the sound of my body thrashing that poor innocent maple as I careened towards the grass.

I felt nothing right away. It was as if my mind was still falling and had not yet caught up to my body. I observed my body crumple into a jumble-puzzle of limbs, torso, head. When I came to myself again, the first sensation was a twinge that shot through the legs and up the spine. I may have cried out. I may have even screamed in fright or pain. But the adrenaline soon subsided. Too soon I was left alone on the grass with my shame and my foolishness. The ache that set into my limbs and joints, and the ennui that set into my spirit as I picked up my briefcase and made my way home, was delicious as chocolate sin cake.

In such a way I embraced and then renounced the art of falling. The ennui continued for a season. But after a while I began to appreciate how remaining upright is also a kind of art. Saying no over and over to the self becomes a kind of yes. It's an old story, no doubt, but one that needs to be retold in every new generation. So: to those of you who secretly yearn for the thrill of the topple, accept this as a cautionary tale. ∎

Here, Alfred Hitchcock

THEY ARE A party of four at a cafe table on the sidewalk of a busy street. The day is warm, but the party is sheltered from the direct mid-day sun by a large umbrella. The slightest breeze blows in off the bay and, with Arnold Palmers all around, the party is comfortable and cheerful. The topic of conversation has turned to the pro basketball playoffs. The two Lakers fans have ganged up on the lone Celtic fan. The fourth member of the party, having no emotional stake in the debate, has begun to goad both sides by identifying the well-known weaknesses in each team's roster.

Unknown to all of them, under the table, strapped with duct tape to the support pole, hidden by the tablecloth, and almost totally silent, ticks the timer of a crudely homemade bomb. It is only minutes from detonation. Who planted the bomb here? Has the timer been set to kill these four in particular, or would any party do? Dear reader, I wish I knew. What an interesting story this might be if I were privy to such juicy motivations. But I'm afraid that, like any mere mortal, my knowledge of the world, even this fictional one, has its limits. I don't know who made the bomb or planted it here. Nor do I know why they did it. I only know that the minutes are ticking away, as minutes will do, while our party of four, who are still hotly engaged in basketball trivia, comfortably sits and sucks their Arnold Palmers through straws, ignorant that the timer holds the secret of their collective demise. All I can do as narrator of this story is return to the action, such as it is.

The argument over whether the great, lumbering, temperamental Laker center will remain healthy throughout the postseason has grown so heated, that one member of the party, in a sweeping gesture, knocks over his Arnold Palmer, spilling the caramel-colored fluid and several ice cubes all over the tablecloth and even into the lap of the lone Celtic fan. Being a Celtic fan apparently isn't humiliation enough; wet trousers now punctuate his social isolation. He stands quickly and grabs the only dry napkin left on the table in a feeble attempt to sop up the chilly mess. In so doing, he accidentally grabs the edge of the tablecloth and yanks.

You can see where this is going now, can't you, reader? As much as the dark twin who occupies that part of your personality Herr Freud identified as the Id would love to see the bomb explode and witness the blood, pain, confusion, and destruction, you sense that I am going to move this story in the direction of the near miss. Or the near hit, depending on your perspective. Now that I have deftly removed the tablecloth and created the potential for the party to discover their peril and so the opportunity to escape doom, who, you might ask, will actually discover the bomb, one of the basketball fans, the waiter, or some alert passerby? It must be one of the party of four. To bring in an outsider to resolve the tension would be to commit the writer's sin of *deus ex machina*, the great flaw of Euripides, whose tragedies have long been criticized for their too easy unravellings of tightly tangled plots.

If the Celtic fan has stood to wipe the iced tea and lemonade from his trousers, then he is above the sight line of the under-the-table explosive device. That takes him out of the running, much as I would like to give him the role of hero after having soaked his lap, poor fellow. That leaves the other three: two Laker fans and one who is above the basketball fray. But here I run into a problem of exposition, for I have not sufficiently developed the individual personalities of the two Laker fans enough to justify making one of them the protagonist here. I would have to stop the forward momentum of the story and provide some prescient backstory in order to evoke the proper amount of sympathy from you, dear reader. And this would no doubt frustrate your enjoyment of the plot to such an extent that you just might give up. For a fiction writer, that is the unpardonable sin.

No, I'm afraid the only justifiable choice for the character to discover the bomb and carry the story from this point to the climax is the witty fourth member, the non-basketball fan. How ironic that it is he who must perform the ultimate slam dunk. Here, no doubt, I have offended all basketball fans who may be reading this story. Well, was it Abraham Lincoln who said you can't please all the people all the time? Or was that rather about fooling all the people all of the time? Pleasing or fooling, we want them both from a fiction, don't we? We might even define fiction as the art of being pleasantly fooled.

But now I'm risking losing all readers—not just basketball fans—because I am theorizing about the art of fiction when I should be practicing it. Very well. Back to our story.

The non-basketball fan bends over to pick up some large shards of broken glass, for the Celtic fan's awkward yank on the tablecloth has sent the drink glasses to the pavement. With his head now under the tabletop, he is eye-level with the explosive device. At first he assumes it is a jerry-rigged electrical hookup, perhaps to power a table lamp or decorative lighting on the umbrella. But a quick glance at the umbrella and the tabletop reveal no decorative lighting whatsoever. Instinctively, he reaches out to touch the device, turning the timer face forward. Seeing the hand of the timer moving around the dial, he recoils in panic, smashing the back of his head against the underside of the table. He lets out a yelp, and then drops to his knees. He lands in some broken glass and lets out another cry.

Why, you may ask, am I employing such standard comic schtick to an otherwise serious story of suspense? I could say that this is a strategic tactic, designed to distract you briefly from the intensity of the moment and add greater delight in the movement of the story toward its inevitable crisis. But it would be closer to the truth for me to say that I simply like this kind of stuff. It never ceases to amuse me when characters whack their heads or trip on a step or catch a body part in a closing door. OK, to be completely honest, neither explanation will do. The honest truth is that such predictable rubbish bores the shit out of me. You see it on the boob tube every day. So why have I included it in my story? I don't know what else to do. Sometimes, no matter how good you are, you reach into the big felt hat and pull out the old familiar rabbit. It's just part of the job.

What can I say? I'm no Tolstoy. I hope I haven't disappointed you so much that you've mentally declared me a hack and are seconds away from giving up on me. I beg of you: give me another chance. As they used to say in the old days, I cry you mercy. Back to the story.

After he recovers single vision and brings himself upright again in his chair, the non-basketball fan grabs the elbow of one of the Laker fans and asks him to look under the table. He does so. "What the hell?" he says, returning upright. The two men look at each other as the waiter rushes over with a broom and a dustpan. The two men ask the waiter for a third opinion. He squats and looks as well, then stands stiffly upright, drops the broom and dustpan, and begins to back away from the table. He has the presence of mind, this young waiter, to pull his cell phone from his pocket and dial 9-1-1. He calmly tells those in the outdoor seating area to calmly move away from the tables. It is one of the Laker fans who panics. "Bomb!" he yells. And then people begin the leaping, bumping, screaming, and outright running for their lives that you might expect for such a scene.

I must stop now and admit that I have borrowed this scenario from Alfred Hitchcock, who used the bomb-under-the-table anecdote to illustrate his theory of how suspense could be communicated using the language of "pure cinema," whatever that may be. I use the term "borrow" here rather than steal because I fully intend to return it again when I'm finished. Hitch, as his Hollywood friends liked to call him, used to say that once you've sprung such a tense situation upon an audience (or, for that matter, a reader), you must never allow the bomb to go off. The innocent people, even these dubious basketball fans, must escape harm, thus "diffusing" the tension. I couldn't resist the bad pun. I promise not to do it again. And so now, dear reader, comes the moment of truth. Do these innocent ones escape harm? I confess I don't have the heart to blow them up. No Quentin Tarantino me. Hitchcock did it once—in *Saboteur*—and forever after declared it "cheating." I tend to side with the old master rather than the young upstart. Call it a character flaw.

The sidewalk cafe sitters, including the waiter, do indeed run clear of the blast. There is, after all, only one bomb, and it is, remember, a crude device. Think what great harm would have been done if the humiliated Celtic fan hadn't accidentally ripped the tablecloth from the table. The pictures of the rubble that would no doubt appear later on the evening news would have to also include pools of blood and stray limbs behind lines of yellow police tape.

The theme of such a story could only be that sometimes the innocent suffer in this world and there's no damn sense or justice in it. Instead, my theme is somewhat less nihilistic. Sometimes, against all odds, good happens. God preserves us. Why? I just don't know. Why not? And now my work is finished. The survivors have a splendid story to tell. In fact, dear reader, I am one of those four survivors. Or am I the waiter? I can't remember. No, of course I'm not the waiter. I must be among the four or else how could I know the details of the story before the waiter enters it? No, neither option can be true, since the plot has been admittedly borrowed. Here I am again, trying to pleasantly fool you.

Here, Alfred Hitchcock, you can have this story back now. It has served my purpose. Let it go on serving yours as well. Someday it will serve someone else. That is the way with stories. We keep passing them around, don't we? As a wise man once said, there's nothing new under the sun. We're all in the recycling business. Let me leave you, reader, with an image that will serve as a resolution: The last bit of debris falls near the two Laker fans, who stand by safely under an awning across the avenue when the bomb finally goes off. One of them brushes the small shards of plastic, glass, wood, and canvas from his shoulders, as he says, "Can you believe that?"

And I'll give the final line to my favorite character—you're not supposed to have favorites among your own children, but I think you'll agree he deserves special mention—the brave, clear-headed waiter, who had the presence of mind to evacuate the cafe in the final seconds before the blast. The young man answers, "If I hadn't seen it with my own eyes, no." ▪

The Gill Man in Purgatory

WHEN THEY HEAR about my death by drowning, the other spirits I meet here often gasp, raising phantom hands to phantom mouths. "How harshly ironic," or something to that effect, they sputter. In life, you see, I was the stunt man inside the gill monster suit in the 1954 Universal International picture, *Creature from the Black Lagoon*. I was an excellent swimmer, a two-time Olympic contender; in fact, that's why I was chosen to play the part. You may remember how effortlessly I moved through the swamp in that fifty-pound foam rubber outfit. It was the fins that kept me alive: fins on hands and feet that displaced more water than any mere human could. Those and the regulator that Scotty, the underwater cameraman, shared with me.

It was hot as hell in that foam rubber suit, I can tell you. Long, hot, drippy days I spent on location with the second unit in that torrid Florida swamp, while the above-water cast lounged in air-conditioned dressing rooms on the Universal back lot. The insects were as big as the birds. We'd sit on the porch of the motel at night, swatting at them with empty beer bottles. Five weeks on location at $125 a week. I'm not complaining. What would be the point of that now? Besides, one of the advantages of living on this side of the time and space divide is that here we have no doubt that suffering has a purpose. On that side, those who use the brain that came with their bodies often wonder if suffering isn't just some kind of cosmic joke or just an accident of biology. No, neither. But if I tried to explain what I know, you wouldn't buy it. Not in your condition.

Everyone here is obsessed with ultimate meaning, you see, because there are no fleshly needs or wants to distract us from our metaphysical musing. Like spirit cows forever out to pasture, all we can do is chew and chew on the cud of our lives, swallowing and re-swallowing that which was, that which might have been, and that which is to come. There is more honest theological speculation here than in the best of seminaries.

And here the issues are not just academic. I often overhear passionately framed questions that sum up the frustrations of a lifetime, such as "Why did God allow me to fall so deeply in love with a woman He knew would repeatedly betray me?" Or how about this one: "Why did God bother to let us build up our little town if it was only going to be blown away by a cyclone?" And so on. These questions trip from the phantom lips of the dead as naturally as dandelions sprout in fields of summer grass. What purpose our passion? What function our toil? And so, invariably, after the initial shock of my manner of death wears thin, my fellow spirits will say, "You just have to wonder what the Great Satirist was thinking," or something to that effect.

As I said before, I could try to explain where these spiritual bitch and whine sessions lead, but I'd just be wasting your time. Such knowledge attracted Eve and her erstwhile partner in crime, as the story is told, and you remember where it got them: stuck in a place not too different from this one. I can safely tell you this much, however: I dwell within sight of the cool light of heaven; it's just out there beyond the tree line that separates this place from His presence.

I'll tell you something else about that gill man gig. I still dream about it. You may be surprised to hear that we spirits dream. We have the most vivid dreams you can imagine. Oh, to have a body again! Even a body trapped in a foam rubber monster suit twenty feet down in a murky Florida swamp. I beg of you, enjoy such torments while you can. I speak as one whose envy has yet to burn away. Now, my lust, gone. Even as I recall the beautiful body double for Julie Adams, the woman I pursued in my cinematic underwater fiefdom, I feel no stirrings. No loins, no stirrings. You'd be surprised how easily some of our most besetting sins drop away with the body. Gluttony, greed, sloth: gone, gone, gone. It's the intellectual habits that linger — your envy, your pride. These are the greatest hits of the seven deadlies.

And here, of course, is another subject to occupy us during our long theological phantom jaw sessions. Why, oh Lord, were we allowed to wallow so long and so helplessly in our own filth? Again, you wouldn't like the answer. As prisoners of flesh and blood, hormones and chance, you'd likely head for the highest window in your neighborhood and take a flying leap. Believe me, that wouldn't help. You'd only end up with way too much time to contemplate that terrible, wonderful flight.

The angels are a good source of information. I think they are allowed to tell us things here that will prompt the long process of purgation, move us along in our spiritual peristalsis. Many, many of us have issues with patience. Yes, and plenty of anger to be burned away here, too. Lots and lots of anger . . . it spurts out like phantom geysers, sulphuric spiritual farts that have a way of lingering in this dry and brittle land like a skunk's emissions on a clear summer's night.

There was a spirit here who laughed outright at my fate. It was a laugh dripping in anger. He was only recently dead himself, killed by a shotgun blast in a convenience store robbery attempt. The cashier he pointed his handgun at held a Remington 1100 beneath the counter. The angel who fetched him told me he'd never seen a man laugh like that at the sight of his own bloody corpse as he left it lying on the linoleum and entered the famous blue tunnel towards, well, this place. So I suppose I shouldn't be shocked that he laughed at me. And in a way I guess my own death has its amusing angle. The big bad gill man, half fish, half human, amphibious wonder of evolution, trips on his own flip-flops on the edge of his suburban swimming pool, twists his ankle, falls into the deep end, hitting his temple on the edge of his new diving board on the way in. The angels have shown me the scene in slow-motion, and I must admit it does have a certain Chaplinesque flair. And I guess I emitted a wry giggle myself upon viewing it. You can do that here. An almost uniformly sober subject on the carnal side of the divide, here the cross between worlds is understood as a simple sidestep into another realm.

Nevertheless — a gun blast, a konk on the head — neither of us was ready to leave. Neither of us was ready for heaven. Luckily, neither of us went to hell. I'm told there is a woman here who passed close enough to hear a demon whisper a vulgarism in her ear. You'd think we'd all be more separated out. But, no, like I said, we can see heaven from where we are, on a clear day. They're all clear days beyond the tree line. By the way, from here the trees appear to be eucalyptus, those tall, fragrant Australian beauties. I only wish I had a real nose to enjoy them with.

I've heard through the phantom grapevine that one soul here has been burning his way through this rocky landscape for three and a half centuries. Apparently there is no one on the solid side who remembers him. It is in part the prayers of the living that calibrate our progress toward that heavenly tree line. I'm told (though I'm not close enough to actually report this from experience) that a joyful cry goes up whenever one of us crosses into paradise. I imagine it sounds something like the angelic version of a home team NFL touchdown in the final seconds of a come-from-behind victory.

Unhinged as I am from time and space, my mind freely visits the moments of my enfleshment. There are three key moments that haunt me nearly continuously. The first is the warm and watery isolation tank of my mother's womb. There I first became aware of my own hands and feet, webbed as they were then and, strangely, were to be again. It wasn't all peace and warm goo, however. My mother loved spicy food. The chili peppers in her tamales—a pregnancy craving she could not deny—sent my developing nervous system into spasms not unlike minor electrical charges.

The second moment is the experience of swimming with ease through the swamp in my famous foam rubber suit. The webbed gloves and flippers gave me a delirious feeling of freedom. Here again there were moments of discomfort, the occasional sense of panic when, completely out of breath, I reached for the cameraman's regulator after a particularly long take. A time or two I simply ripped the front of the mask off to get at it, sucking air as I had once sucked milk from my mother's breast.

And third is, of course, the moment of my death, as I tripped (and now continue to trip over and over in my mind, which is all that is left me) on my stupid flip-flops, twisted my stupid ankle . . . down and down I went, again and again, hitting my stupid head on the edge of my brand-spanking-new fiberglass diving board. The good news: the pain passed in an instant.

The loved ones I left behind have thanked God, as have I, for this small mercy. I was only semi-conscious as I sank and sank to the bottom, gently resting there for several minutes (exactly twelve minutes and thirty-five seconds) before the young firefighter pulled me from the water and began his noble but futile effort to revive me. By then I was well into my blue tunnel experience, and there was no way I was coming back.

I can also report this to you, though it is one thing to hear how this works and another altogether to experience: since we are beyond time and space here, these moments—and all moments—are simultaneous. It is all one, you see, which is to say that while I am floating in my mother's womb I am also swimming in the swamp just beneath the body double in the bathing suit and I am also sinking to my death at the bottom of the deep end of my suburban pool. Another irony: you may remember that the final shot of *Creature* shows me, after having pulled the scientist's harpoon from my back, sinking to the bottom of the Amazonian lagoon. Up comes the moody monster music. Cue the jungle noises. Roll the credits on my life. Mommy, mommy, no more chili peppers, please. Somewhere beyond the sweet-scented tree line, the Great Satirist is covering His great mouth with His hand. Is that a grin or a smirk He's hiding? ∎

The Miracula of Chumley Barker

I NEVER KNEW HIM. In the interest of full disclosure I must begin with this simple fact. I never met the man. Still, I feel I know him better today than I know myself. To the uninitiated, this is perhaps a stumbling block. Believe me, I know how strange it sounds. How could I claim to know someone I never met? Impossible. And yet.

Others have tried to write about this; some of them have done a good job, a faithful job, with what they knew. But they only told bits and pieces of the story. So I have done some research and attempted here to reconstruct as much of the actual story as possible. I write this so you can decide for yourself if it is true, truth of course being in the mind of the beholder.

One day I received in the mail from an anonymous source a human thumb contained in a small jewelry case. The note inside the box said only, "Chum's thumb. Handle with care. Pass along to the next needy loser after you have been helped out of your troubles." Naturally I was shocked and not a little repulsed. Which of my friends was sick enough to pull a prank like this? The thing was: I happened to be a needy loser when the thumb arrived in my mailbox. In fact, it arrived on the worst day in a two-week losing streak that had me wondering if I was to be the twenty-first-century Job.

I won't tell all the juicy details of my strife; this isn't really my story, after all; it's Chum's. Suffice it to say, I had sunk to the sandy bottom of my life. After months of mutual disappointment and then weeks of outright warfare between us, my wife had taken the kids to live with her mother in New Jersey. Three days later I lost the best job I'd ever had in a massive company lay-off. A week after that, the bank notified me that my house had gone into foreclosure. In this I wasn't alone; hundreds of thousands of us had been sucked into loans we could never repay by a system run amuck. But no system had twisted my arm and forced me to sign the papers to a mortgage I knew I could never pay off. And so serious depression had set in. I was self-medicating with a bottle of vodka a day and the complete films of Woody Allen on Netflix. I was due for a check up, but I avoided the doctor for fear he would find cancer.

A few days later the thumb arrived.

I had just finished watching *Crimes and Misdemeanors*. I was about to give up on Woody Allen because it occurred to me about halfway through the film that what he was doing was remaking the same film year after year. The *Crimes and Misdemeanors* year was a particularly good year by the Woody Allen calendar. But I was a bit dizzy from all the whining and self-analysis, the feeble attempts to elevate tawdry plot twists by attaching them to inflated themes. And why must every character in a Woody Allen film sound so much like Woody? You get my mood. The bottle of Smirnoff's I was nursing wasn't helping. I had already cycled through being a numb drunk to a silly drunk to an angry drunk. I was quickly becoming a morose drunk. I was lying on my couch in my soon-to-be-the-bank's living room when I saw the postman walk by lugging his big satchel. You know it's a bad sign when the only thing you have to look forward to in your life is the daily mail.

The nice thing about hitting bottom is, well . . . it's the bottom. Like Job sitting on the pile of ashes, you know at that point that things can only get better. Or stop altogether. In fact, as I was lying there on the couch watching the postman pass, I was thinking of a painless way to make it stop altogether. Closing the garage door with the car running topped my list. As I stumbled out to the mailbox, I was considering how long it would take for the carbon monoxide fumes to overtake me. I had always heard that carbon monoxide caused delightfully goofy hallucinogenic dreams. In my mind's eye I was constructing some sweet Peter Max-inspired images as I pulled the mail from the box and halted back to the house. Minutes later, I was staring down at the thumb in the small jewelry box, the black velvet-covered sort of box that watches used to come in before they started coming in those tacky plastic things.

Let me get straight to the point: Chum's thumb worked like a charm. I lay the open jewelry box on my bedroom dresser. I touched the thumb. Well, why not? It sounds pretty gross, I know. But put yourself in my shoes for a moment. To someone who's lost everything that's important to him, petting a human thumb is not such an odd thing. I had carried around a rabbit's foot for a few weeks as a kid. It hung on a small chain on a belt loop until the chain broke during a flag football game and was lost forever in the mud and grass of my junior high school field. I had rubbed that rabbit's foot for luck. So maybe that's where I got the idea. Rub the thumb. So rub I did.

Next morning I received a call from a woman who had worked in the same department as me and had been dumped by the company on the same day. She admitted that she had had a crush on me for years, and now she felt she had nothing to lose by letting me know about it because she had heard through the grapevine that my wife had left. This was a woman I had admired and secretly lusted after. You don't need all the details, but I can tell you that she called on a Tuesday and by Friday we were on our second date and already starting to talk about the wedding. Shortly after rubbing Chum's thumb, I pushed off the sandy bottom and paddled toward the surface again.

Today, that woman is my second wife. Together we went into business doing more or less the same kind of work we had done for our previous employer, but because we had no overhead and no fear, we were able to succeed where our employer had failed by getting bogged down in regulations that only applied to large corporations. Traveling light and avoiding needless expenses, we soon had a client list that rivaled small companies in the same field. So charm it certainly was, that disembodied thumb.

And now, to substantiate this admittedly anecdotal claim, allow me to add the results of my research: His name was Chum, short for Chumley. The only other people who bore the name were butlers in old black-and-white movies. He never shook the hand of another actual, three-dimensional Chumley. And he had been called Chum for so long — as long as he could remember — that he often forgot his full name until he glanced at his driver's license, tax form, or other official document.

Aside from the rarified name, little else about Chum was unique. He was an ordinary man of ordinary stature: neither tall nor short, handsome nor ugly, fat nor thin. All of my sources report that he was upright, well-adjusted, and for the most part, normal. Normal is not the most fashionable word to use these days — who's to say what's normal, after all? — but I think you know what I mean. Some say his personality was bland, but he was interesting enough to have found a wife while in college (though she left him two years later), smart enough to have landed a stable job in the R & D unit of a large computer company, and if he was not attractive, well, at least he was not repulsive — that is, he emitted no unusual odors, displayed no noticeable physical defects, and kept regular habits of good hygiene and mental acuity. In fact, his first thirty years were mostly uneventful. He seemed to blend in to ordinary society in every way.

But in the summer of his thirty-first year, everything changed. He began to gain weight. He grabbed the extra flesh around his waist and wondered at its sudden appearance. At approximately one pound per week, his gain seemed moderate at first. But by the end of the year his paunch was not only noticeable but prominent. His gait slowed; his mood darkened. It wasn't long before he wore only velour sweat suits and fur-lined slippers. The health problems that accompany obesity became his health problems: diabetes, high blood pressure, high cholesterol, sleep apnea, angina. He grew fast as a zucchini in a summer garden. Despite attempts at portion control and exercise, the fat clung to him until he lost hope. I have asked my personal physician what might have triggered such a quick shift in metabolism, and he merely shrugged. Chum did not suddenly become more sedentary in his lifestyle. His diet did not change substantially.

He did not dip into a languid depression. The usual blood tests showed it was not a thyroid condition. Nevertheless he did, as they say, begin to pack on the pounds. The why of it remains something of a mystery. But this part of his story is essential: you must picture him now as perfectly trim and normal, and then, well, there's no other word that will do: obese. It wasn't long until he crossed the threshold of morbid obesity. I could give you the actual weight in pounds, but why press the issue? You get the idea.

Too large to do much else, he sank at first into a soft sofa, and eventually he lay propped in a large bed. In his thirty-second year, he had become an invalid, what people in more indelicate times used to call a shut-in. All day he watched the talk shows. Friends and relatives brought him food and helped him to the toilet. Soon he could no longer fit into the shower. A nurse came in to sponge him and change the sheets and deliver his medications and CPAP supplies. It wasn't long before his friends stopped coming by.

Family members checked in via email. It was difficult for them to be in his presence. It wasn't simply the body odor or the aura of deep sadness (though both were prevalent), but Chum didn't have much to offer in the way of conversation. And often in the middle of a discussion he would simply nod off. Here, at this point, perhaps in response to his social isolation, my sources tell me, he did indeed fall into a deep depression. His life became a dull daily rhythm of eating and watching television, broken only by the visits of two dedicated nurses, who attended him wearing surgical masks and latex gloves. But even they could not resist the need to release the pent-up stress they experienced in his constant care. Behind his back, they referred to him as Jabba the Hutt.

On a popular TV talk show one autumn afternoon, there appeared a man who had won a contest on a reality show for losing the most weight. Diet and exercise were the methods of his liberation from the prison of fat, he said; however, mental discipline was the key that unlocked the cell and allowed his skinny self out. That was the way he told the story, as if there were two of him: a skinny self and a fat self. For years, the man declared, his fat self had kept his skinny self in lock-down. The turning point came when his skinny self said to his fat self: Be gone! He had simply willed it, and his body conformed to his will. What advice did he have, asked the talk show host, for those who were watching at home? Will it, the man said. Picture yourself skinny, and simply make it so.

Chum lay on his bed, partially sunken into the mattress, his body a great conglomeration of mounds and rolls. He turned off the television. He developed a picture in his mind of himself skinny. "I will it," he whispered. No tears of contrition rolled down his fat cheeks and jowls. His conversion was sudden but not necessarily dramatic.

Nothing changed immediately. He finished the double cheeseburger that he had on his side table. But somewhere in his brain a switch had been flipped. That's the way he would later tell the story. A switch flipped, and from then on his skinny self was in control.

And here I must interject that my sources conflict. His mother was said to report that the switch had been flipped as the result of fervent and dedicated prayer; what followed was an inspiring story of personal devotion. His next-door neighbor believed that he had secretly ordered an illegal diet drug from a pharmacy in Mexico; what followed was yet another version of the sad, familiar story of addiction. Other sources tell of a secret Candomble ritual performed in his backyard on the night of a full moon, involving decapitated roosters and the drinking of their blood. These voices do not appear in mainstream tellings; rather, they occupy its conspiratorial fringes. Nevertheless, I offer them for your consideration since they appear in multiple sources.

According to what I now consider the mainstream tradition, the shedding of pounds was a slow, steady process, and not at all easy. But since the skinny self was calling the shots, his fat self had no choice but to obey. He ate a little less at first, and then a lot less, and then only vegetables, a little fish, a little wine, and water, lots of water. The water began to flush his system. That's the way he would later tell it. The water flushed the fat out; the wine buoyed his spirit. Soon his problems were loose skin and excess energy. He could shower again and walk without pain. He was spotted jogging around the neighborhood at night. He sent the nurses away. He bought a new bed and had the old saggy bed hauled away. (Pictures of the old bed have recently been posted on a web site maintained by an organization describing itself as The Disciples of Chum. The caption beneath the photo claims that the bed was found in the local junkyard shortly after his passing and hauled up into the attic of a friend of Chums' ex-wife.)

Within a year he was back to the where he had started, weightwise. His friends and neighbors reconnected. Family members proudly posed for pictures with him. It was at this time that those who knew him best began to talk about the glow. Some described it as a vivid lavenderish aura about the head and neck. Some described it in no uncertain terms as a halo.

Also at this time the stories about his levitation began to circulate. According to his next-door neighbor, he walked into Chum's room one morning and found him floating above the bed. He was asleep—snoring, in fact—but floating several inches off the mattress. An alternate version has one nurse still present, standing upon Chum's bed, pushing him downward with all her weight, in an attempt to get his body back onto the surface of the bed. His body was relaxed but unrelenting; she could not force him to descend again to the mattress. She ran to get a witness, the next-door neighbor, Phil Campbell by name, and when the two of them returned they found him awake and sitting upright on the mattress. He had no memory of the incident and merely giggled when the nurse conveyed the eerie details to him.

The skinny switch stayed on. Chum didn't know how to turn it off. In fact, he didn't really want to turn it off. He wanted to see how far things would go. One of the few surviving quotes from this stage of the story records him as saying, "Let's just see how far this will go." At one point he had surgery to remove the folds of skin that refused to tighten. His cheeks began to sink as though he were constantly sucking lemons. He had to stop eating fish, which made him feel bloated. He could eat a few nuts with effort, but mostly it was green leafy vegetables and the occasional mashed potato. Everything else came right back up. Soon all foods disgusted him. Eventually it was only wine and a little water.

In his thirty-third year, he had to go back to wearing sweat suits and slippers. The velour draped over him like the tattered clothing on a scarecrow fashioned from old broom handles. Eventually he was so bone-thin that he could do nothing but sit again propped on his new bed, in which he hardly made a dent. He watched the talk shows. He let his beard grow. The health problems of the emaciated became his health problems: iron and vitamin deficiencies, lack of bone density, frailty, blurred vision, lack of energy. One strain of memory says he was listless, bored, depressed. Another strain says he was focused, wise, radiant. His doctor tried to hospitalize him; Chum refused. At some point the doctor told him to put his affairs in order.

On the first Saturday afternoon in the month of May, he called in friends and family for the final visit; he had them stand around the edge of the bed. The priest came in and anointed him with oil, performing the rite of extreme unction. Everybody held hands and prayed for him. After the "Amen," he took each person by the hand and looked each in the eyes as he plucked off a piece of himself as a memento. Here there is uniform testimony; all sources report the exact same activity. To his brother he gave an ear, to his next-door neighbor, Phil, an index finger. To his mechanic he gave a knee-cap, to his barber he gave his nose. To his beloved third grade teacher he gave his tongue, which she accepted only after he slipped it into a zip-sealed plastic baggie. One by one they came forth and accepted pieces of Chum; he graciously distributed himself until there lay on the bed only a loose configuration of mute, stray body parts. Two of the eyewitnesses present for the ceremony report that those body parts formed the shape of a heart against the white sheets. Not a drop of blood was shed.

According to instructions Chum had given beforehand, the nurse scooped up the remains in the sheets and took them to the funeral home, where they were passed through the oven and poured into an urn. His mother took the urn with her onto a privately-chartered airplane and, when they were a mile out to sea, on cue from the pilot, she poured them through a funnel in the bottom of the cockpit. The pilot played Chum's favorite song through some headphones. And what was that song? It was Norman Greenbaum's "Spirit in the Sky."

Just so, Chumley Barker gave himself away.

Months later Chum's parts showed up at garage sales and church bazaars throughout the county. Occasionally you would see some teeth on display in a glass case, or a few strands of hair in an envelope marked "Chum's forelock." Someone at the community college flea market had an eyeball for sale. It certainly looked like one of Chum's eyes. His ex-wife received a box in the mail one day marked "Chum's nuts," and for all she knew that may in fact have been what those two slimy, pinkish-brown egg-shaped things were. They disappeared from her freezer not long after. They have not resurfaced.

I must conclude that someone at that final gathering was given the thumb which I received in the mail and which, I believe, triggered the reversal of my own sad state of misfortune. I don't know how many people had possessed it before me. I can tell you that once it had worked its magic in my own life, I began to look around for another needy loser to pass it on to. The details of my search and the identity of the individual to whom I gifted that thumb shall die with me when I join Chum in the sweet bye and bye. I haven't even told them to my beloved second wife, whose love sustains me now and always in the spirit of Chumley Barker.

It was only about eighteen months or so later that a small book of Chum's sayings was published by a local copy center that had once printed business cards for Chum.

They were professionally printed, these numbered sayings, and stapled on the fold like a poetry chapbook. The front cover showed a somewhat blurry photo of Chum lying on his bed in his velour sweat suit. The expression on his face was not quite a smile. It certainly wasn't a frown. The letters across the top said, "The Wisdom of Chum." (Copies are available at The Disciples of Chum web site. Pay-Pal and major credit cards accepted.)

At regular meetings now, we who have been renewed and transformed, read from these sayings, sing along with Norman Greenbaum on the original vinyl Reprise record of "Spirit in the Sky," listen to the testimonies of those present who have come into contact with Chums' body parts, and ruminate a bit on the meaning of those experiences. As you might imagine, the first Saturday in May is a very special day in our little community. I can't tell you the details of the ritual that has developed. On that I have sworn an oath. However, it won't be long now until the delicate privacy of our gatherings is breached.

Lately the meetings have begun to attract local media attention. Word is spreading. People have begun to gain and lose weight for no discernible reason. Stories are circulating about how Chum's parts have led to physical healing, to peace of mind after great personal upheaval, and even to, in Florida, sudden wealth: one of Chum's toenails, used to scratch a lottery ticket there, resulted in a ten-million-dollar prize.

Already, however, the primary sources of Chumley Barker's story have begun to die off, grow silent, or disappear under strange circumstances. And that is why, in part, I have taken it upon myself to compile the facts as we know them and tell the story all in one lump. I never knew the man, yet I touched his thumb and my life was forever changed.

Who knows what miracles are yet to be wrought in his name? I can't begin to guess. I only know that here and now, my life is buoyant; I am filled with an inner peace that sustains me even on the roughest of days. My lovely wife says of our lives that we are gliding on a straight track and rolling along on greased rails. And we know that when we die, Chumley Barker is going to recommend us to the spirit in the sky. When we die and they lay us to rest, we're going to go to the place that's the best. ∎

Creation Story

I STOOD AT DAWN on the eastern shore of the lake with the sun just beginning to top the shoulders of the mountains. After a restless night, I had slipped out of bed and left my wife asleep. I had pulled on yesterday's clothes, silently shut the door behind me, and walked until I reached the water's edge. Now here I stood, looking out at the deep blue water as it shimmered in the morning light. The sky was freckled with cumulus. The mountains that ringed the giant lake were covered with tall ponderosa pine. Huge boulders lay everywhere along the shore. The air was crisp and clean and invigorating.

Surrounded by such grand and primal beauty, you might think that I would be at peace. But my mind was filled with terrifying, obsessive thoughts. Irrational thoughts. Would my car veer over a cliff? Would one of the frequent mountain electrical storms skewer me with a bolt of lightening? Would my wife poison me at dinner tonight? Many people entertained such thoughts; I nurtured them. My will, it seemed, was useless when it came to combating them. The more I tried to release these thoughts, the tighter their grip on me.

So I kicked off my shoes, emptied my pockets into the pebbles at water's edge, and walked in until the water was deep enough to dive. Was I thinking of suicide? Not directly. Through no conscious process at all, my mind sent me one, and only one, clear message: swim across the lake. Had I stopped to consider the idea, I would soon have realized that the lake was too cold and too big for me to possibly cross. But on an unconscious level, I must have concluded that swimming the lake was the only thing that would pull my mind, if only for a while, from its constant sucking on fear's teat.

The initial shock of cold awoke every nerve in my body. It took all of my energy to move my limbs in the freestyle motion, kicking and stroking,

87

kicking and stroking. It wasn't long before I was ducking beneath the buoy line and moving out into the flow of small boat traffic. You should have seen the shocked look on the faces of those early morning speedboat drivers and jet ski riders as they came upon me. They slowed and politely asked if I needed to be rescued. I shook my head and continued. Am I a good swimmer? Not really. But I know how it's done.

One of the teenagers on a jet ski turned to his companion on another jet ski and asked, "Can he do that?" His friend only shrugged. "It's a free country," he said. "Maybe he's some kind of Olympic dude." This answer seemed to satisfy them, so they zoomed on.

Soon the speedboat engines and the laughter of skiers faded. I was out in deeper water now. The wind sculpted a choppy series of small waves. Was it only my imagination that the water was even colder now? And somehow more viscous? A few yachts passed close enough to hail me. One of them, a big white vessel called *Princess of the Lake*, slowed next to me.

A group of men and women in polo shirts and ball caps gaped at me from the railing on the deck. They held up their martini glasses as if to toast my efforts. Someone tossed a lifesaver into the water in front of me. "Grab the buoy," a voice said over a loudspeaker, "We'll bring you in." Was that my wife there at the railing, standing next to a tall, handsome man, gray at the temples but otherwise fit and trim? The sun was so bright above their heads now I couldn't get a second look. Spots danced before my sight.

I treaded water a moment, considering. Dry clothes and a dry martini awaited. All I had to do was grab hold. Soon I could be standing on the deck of the *Princess of the Lake*. The friendly but incredulous people in polo shirts and ball caps would pat me on the back and say, "My God, man, what were you thinking? Lucky we came along, eh?" And if that was my wife up there, she might want to embrace me; she might have even hired the yacht to come out after me. But how could she have known that I had gone for a swim? Had someone already discovered my clothes along the bank?

The voice over the loudspeaker boomed again, this time more insistently, "Grab the buoy!"

I was tired and cold. Was the sun already straight overhead? Had I been in the lake half a day already? I put my head back into the water and continued swimming. I pushed the buoy out of my way and flipped over on my back, showing off my backstroke. I waved as casually as I could. The people at the railing were gesticulating now, pointing to the buoy and shouting. I tried to make it clear to them that I was all right. I swam on. The yacht floated in place until I was out of vocal range. Then I heard the engines start up again.

It was here — somewhere, if I had to guess, near the middle of the lake — that I began to think of monsters. They were not a typical part of my obsessive repertoire. My usual list of irrational fears were all based in real things and possible events, not the mythic or legendary. But here I began to envision huge serpentine leviathans moaning and twirling in the depths below me. They didn't last long, these ancient fears; in fact, they may have been the last gasps of the sickness I was beginning to leave behind.

I grew more tired and more cold. How long had I been going? My watch lay in the pebbles next to my shoes. I had been swimming for years. In fact, I couldn't now remember my life before I dove into this frigid, clear water. All I had ever done was kick and throw my arms and turn my head. I could see the mountains in the distance begin to close in. The lake grew darker in color, and I realized it was the shadow of these mountains as the sun began to dip behind the western peaks.

My muscles began to cramp, especially the legs. I cherished the cramps. The ache in my side became an old friend. And then the numbness began. My legs appeared to be doing the work I wanted them to do, kicking more or less of their own accord, only I could no longer feel them as part of my body. I know it sounds funny to say, but it was around this time that I believe I may have fallen asleep, or gone into some kind of stupor. At any rate, the loud siren and the flashing light on the rescue boat had the effect of an alarm clock.

The sleek red jet boat eased alongside me. Eager, athletic young men pulled on wet suits. One of them in some sort of uniform was chattering in a foreign tongue through a megaphone. I understand now that it wasn't a foreign tongue at all; probably he was speaking to me in plain old American English, but I was unable to process it. Most probably he was calmly reassuring me that they would have me out of the water momentarily, that I would soon be safe and sound and dry and warm.

Two of the young men dove into the water. For a moment I imagined they were a pair of large seals who had come to play. But they began to poke and prod at me, to force their arms around my torso and pull me toward the boat. I don't know where I found the strength to fight them off. If a person doesn't want to be rescued, no amount of good intentions can make it happen. I looked up into the darkening sky. I drew deep breaths. I imagined myself a creature of the deep who had come to the surface to see what all the fuss was about. I pushed them away, kicked at them, and simply out-swam them. Olympic dude, I thought, again and again. I'm an Olympic dude.

Soon the boat was right alongside and some sort of metal device was in the water, attempting to hook me like a big old fish and haul me aboard. They scolded me harshly in their foreign tongue. They made it clear that they were willing to die in the service of my rescue. At one point I swam beneath their boat. It was then, I think, they must've reasoned that the effort was futile. Or perhaps they decided that if I had that much energy I might just make it to the western shore under my own power. Whatever. The point is they stopped harassing me and drove their sleek boat back out toward the center of the lake, leaving me huffing and puffing, stroking my aching arms and kicking my numb legs despite their heroism.

All fear was gone. In a sense, all thought was gone. I now swam in a substance that only weeks before had covered the mountains in a glorious white sheen. I can tell you this: I grew bigger with every stroke, stronger with every kick. A helicopter hovered overhead. And then another. Or was it the same copter back for another look? For a time I hovered over my body with it, looking down at my own body, now gray and scaly and huge. What sort of creature had I become?

Very soon after this, the noise of the helicopter faded and the whole earth grew silent. Then I heard water lapping the shore up ahead of me.

Directly beneath me, through forty or so feet of crystal clear water, was a village of sunken cabins. They stood much as they had a hundred years before, when the lake was smaller and they overlooked its western shore. I saw chimneys and bicycles and a tireless tractor and even sunken trees without leaves. What sort of music was that I heard, drifting up to the surface? Fiddles and guitars, I believe. The cabins passed beneath me as if I were a low-flying plane passing over the village.

When I lifted my head I saw the huge ponderosa pines looming before me along the shoreline. It wasn't long before my feet touched pebbles, and I stood again. I was shivering. My skin was a grayish-blue color; it tingled. I could feel the wind in my hair, which had grown long and thin. I could smell a fire on the breeze. My toes were webbed and my hands looked like paddles.

There I stood at dusk on the opposite shore, looking back across the lake, now half-covered in shadow, looking back across the watery path of my synchronized swim with the sun. Overhead the cumulus clouds had turned a pinkish-orange as the sun sank behind the trees along the ridgeline.

No one came to greet me. Not a soul welcomed me into my new life. I beg your pardon: the moon was up. The crickets were alert and cheerful. And as I said, my fear was gone. Somewhere along the line, it had leapt from my back and lit out on its own. I imagine it is still floating out there in the middle of the lake. Some mornings early, as I crouch eating a trout for breakfast on the promontory, I think I see it bobbing in the wake of the ski boats and the yachts.

I cannot recommend this if your desire is to live again among people. I can only say that if you are called to the shore of a clear mountain lake and hear a singular voice bidding you to come, and if you cannot with all your reason or imagination bring yourself to decline, then you won't be sorry.

There are those on the eastern shore who would label my story an apocalypse. Let them. It is time for those of us who have stories like this to tell, strange stories that throttle us even as we tell them, to go ahead and bear witness. ∎

Hemingway's Juvenalia

IT WAS A small leather valise and it was stuffed with manuscripts. It was not the kind of valise constructed of high-quality leather and dark, polished straps with brass initials on the side. It was a simple case made of ordinary materials with a single leather strap that buckled over the top like a good belt. His wife had packed all that he had written in the past three years into the case. There were stories and there were poems and there was the germ of a novel. She was bringing them to her husband so he could show them to a man who wanted to see her husband's work. The man admired her husband's writing and knew some editors and publishers back in the states who might be interested in something new. Her husband was writing articles on a peace conference in Lausanne for a Canadian newspaper. The work was not the kind he would choose for himself, but he had a wife to support, and six articles would pay another six months rent on their Montparnasse flat.

When she stepped off the train in Lausanne she had to tell her husband that the valise had been stolen, probably before the train ever left the Paris station. She stiffened her spine as she walked down the steps, embraced him, and tried to speak clearly. She refused to wipe the tears as they rolled down her cheeks. Finally he took his handkerchief and daubed them. Worse things had happened to them both. Worse still would occur in the not-too-distant future. But at the time it was happening, it was the hardest journey she had ever made; it was the toughest news he had ever had to receive.

THE THIEF STEPPED off the train and walked swiftly up the platform toward the street. He exited through a side door of the Gare de Lyon, crossed the Boulevard Diderot, and turned up a familiar alley, stepping into the kitchen of the cafe in which his brother-in-law worked as a waiter. He opened the valise, pulled out the papers, and searched the side pockets. The papers contained gibberish in what appeared to be English. Since the war, Paris had been lousy with English. You heard it in the cafes and in the bars. You heard it in the patisseries and in the flower shops. He stuffed the papers into the kitchen incinerator, opened the flue, and pulled the lever. The incinerator filled with flames and the ashes rose up the flue, emerging from the chimney pot and floating into the cool air over the rooftops of Rue Abel.

The thief examined the valise for any identifying features. Finding none, he tucked it under his arm and stepped back into the alley. He tightened the scarf around his neck. The young woman who had placed the valise so gingerly beneath her seat had treated it with such care that he thought for certain it would have money in it. He cursed her. The stupid bitch was one of those worthless Americans who sipped brandy all day in the cafes of Montparnasse and fancied themselves writers. He had done the world a favor this morning by saving it from the romantic drivel of another English-speaking hack.

THE BASTARD HAD stepped between them. The thief had taken the valise right from under her stupid little nose and now the ending had begun. He thought it had begun back in Paris, in the weeks leading up to the trip. The apartment had grown small and their moods — they were both to blame for it, he admitted that — had grown large. But now it seemed, in hindsight, that those weeks were the last throes of the romance, such as it was, and now the ending had begun in earnest. He felt silly: here he was at a peace conference, after all, writing reports for the Toronto paper about desiccated old men talking and endlessly talking about peace, and here war had broken out between he and Hadley. Hadley, the only woman who had broken the time-honored barrier between lover and friend, for she had been both. And now, it seemed, she was neither. It made him slightly sick to think of it, but the picture of them living apart, of taking completely separate lives began to form in his imagination. Perhaps he would go back to Spain in the spring. Alone. He would fish in the cold streams and he would drink anise in the bodegas and he would watch the bulls. Spain would not be medicine for him this time, however — only a temporary anesthetic, something to dull the pain as the wounds closed.

He went out for a long walk while Hadley unpacked her bag. He needed to walk off the anger so as not to take it all out on Hadley. She did not deserve that. It was a thief, after all, who snatched the valise. He had snatched many others that week, no doubt, and would snatch many more before the gendarmes would finally catch him.

He just needed to walk and let the cold Swiss air fill his lungs and clear his mind. She had looked at him like a child when she stepped off the train platform. Her eyes had welled and her lip had quivered. She looked like a waif who had been dismissed from school and had to face her disgruntled parents. That was all he was to her now, a stern and disappointed father. And part of him would always think of her as a child who had somehow let him down and whom he could never somehow forgive, despite her genuinely contrite heart.

Well, it was gone. That was all. Some of it was good work, too. Perhaps it was very good. But it was gone and that's all there was to it. Pound had dismissed most of it anyway. It was no good chewing it, like a cow returning to his cud. He would walk it off. He would stop for a drink in the hotel bar with his colleague from *The Star*. He would laugh about it and tell the story to the newspaper boys from the states. He would act out the part of the smarmy thief tucking the valise under his arm and shuffling off the train. They would all have a laugh about it while in his mind he pictured the thief moving furtively through the crowds at the Gare de Lyon, melting into the onslaught of people, wondering what his cleverness and his swiftness had got him this time. ∎

Not Talking About the Moon

A SIREN SCREAMED ON the next street over. Lucy awoke suddenly and knew without looking that Gilbert was gone. The neon lights across the alley flooded the bedroom with alternate flashes of red and green lightening. The sheet next to her was damp and smelled salty.

She held out one hand and felt her way along the hall with her fingertips. Her slippers scuffed along the rug. "Gil?" she called out. "Gil, baby, are you all right?" She reached through the doorway and snapped on the bathroom light, squinted from its glare, snapped it off. Her slippers scuffed some more. "Gil?"

"Shhh!"

Lucy stopped in the kitchen archway. "Gil?"

"Here," he whispered. Gilbert sat on the floor next to the refrigerator. A shaft of moonlight shone through the window like a blue spotlight.

"Too hot?" she asked.

"Hot ain't the word," he said.

"The sheets are damp."

"Tell me about it. I would've stayed but I can't swim." He pressed his head against the wall, closed one eye, and peered behind the refrigerator.

"What're you doing?" she asked.

"Shhh!"

"Gil, I will not be shushed in my own house."

"I'm waiting," he said.

Lucy picked the sleep from her eyes. "What are you waiting for?"

"Shhh."

"You want some coffee?"

"I want you to shut up."

"Don't talk like that, baby. I just woke up from a hot sleep. All I want to know is what you're doing."

"Search and destroy."

Lucy snapped on the kitchen light.

Gilbert shielded his eyes and lay back on the linoleum with a groan.

On the floor, next to Gilbert's legs, was a frying pan. And next to the frying pan lay a pancake turner. There was something in the frying pan. Lucy leaned over it. Cockroaches. The pan was half-filled with dead cockroaches of all sizes.

Lucy stepped back. She looked down at Gilbert and the pan of roaches. "Gilbert . . . why?"

"Couldn't sleep."

"You could read."

"I kept tossing. Couldn't relax. I kept thinking about them crawling all over the place out here while we slept in there. Or tried to sleep. The more I thought about it the more it bugged me. After a while, I couldn't stand it."

Lucy looked at the clock on the wall. Three thirty. "So you've been out here all night?"

"I stalked them," he said. "There's one left. A big son of a bitch. Feelers long as my finger. The godfather cockroach."

Lucy looked down into the pan. "Don't you think you've got enough for tonight?"

"Hit the light, will you?" He sat up.

"What?"

"It won't come out with the light on."

"Honey, why don't you let that one go. It's probably so scared now it'll leave—"

"Don't make me laugh. They don't leave. They're territorial, like cats. It won't leave until I kill it."

"Gil. Why are you doing this?"

"I told you."

"You couldn't stop thinking about them. Couldn't you just concentrate on something else? Something nice?"

"I could hear them."

"You can't hear cockroaches."

"I heard them."

"What do they sound like?"

"Like crawling . . . little . . . like rain on the window only softer . . . tick tick tick. Like that only softer. Pretty soon there were millions of little feet going tick tick tick on the Formica." He stood up and snapped off the light.

She heard him move the pan aside, heard the crick in his knee as he squatted down next to the fridge.

"Now I've got to wait for my eyes to adjust," he said.

"You can't hear cockroaches," Lucy said.

As her eyes adjusted, she focused on the pile of roaches in the frying pan. "How many are there?" she asked.

"Eighteen. Nineteen counting this one."

"How do you know that's the last one?"

"I know."

"How?"

"This one's their leader."

"You can't know that."

Gilbert picked up the pancake turner. "I see it," he said.

"Is it coming out?" Lucy asked. She squatted at a safe distance.

"Shhh."

After a long squatted silence her ankles began to give way. She had to move. Lucy picked up the frying pan by the handle.

"Leave them be," Gilbert whispered.

"What're you going to do with them?" Lucy whispered. She set the pan back on the floor with a loud clink.

"Ahhh!" Gilbert cried.

"What?"

"It went underneath." Gilbert sat back. He moved the frying pan closer to the fridge.

"You want some coffee?" she asked.

"When my brother came home from Vietnam he told us about these guys who would cut the heads off gooks and stick them on top of poles."

"Why?"

"To instill fear."

"Gilbert—"

"Know what a cockroach dies of if you cut off its head? Guess."

"I don't want to guess."

"Starvation," he said. "If it could only find some way to eat, it would go on living without a head."

"How is that possible?" she asked.

"They're invincible. They're prehistoric. Been here for millions of years. I saw something about it on TV."

Lucy grasped the handle of the pan and shook the dead roaches around like popcorn. "What're you going to do with them?"

Gilbert smiled. "You'll see."

"I'm making some coffee. You want some?"

"Ice it," he said.

Lucy put the coffee on. Gilbert went to the sink and splashed cold water on his face. Then he went to the window. After a few minutes, she brought him a tall glass of iced coffee. They stood at the window looking out.

Several lights were on in the apartment building across the street. Most people had their windows open; some slept out on their narrow balconies, the mild nighttime traffic sputtering below them.

Gilbert said, "Pretty soon we'll all be gone. All of those people there. Us. Dead and gone. Probably just the cockroaches left. They'll be living in our homes without us to interrupt their lives."

"That's a pretty thought," Lucy said.

"You don't get it, do you?" Gilbert asked.

"I get it," she answered. "It's a hot night. My mom used to call that a witches' moon. Its light throws a curse on people. It makes them despair. Look at all those people sweating it out over there, just like us."

"I'm not talking about the moon," he said.

"Yes you are."

Lucy grabbed his arm. "Gil," she said, looking back into the kitchen. The long feelers of the big cockroach were waving around at the edge of the fridge. Its head peeked out.

Gilbert grabbed the pancake turner and slipped to the floor. He scooted up near the fridge on his elbows and in one quick motion flicked the roach out from under the fridge with the pancake turner. The roach wheeled into the center of the floor and scrambled beneath the pan.

Gilbert smiled at Lucy. He picked up the pan with one hand and came down with the pancake turner in the other. He disabled the roach with the first blow, killed it with the second, then scooped up the corpse and slipped it into the pan along with its dead comrades.

Gilbert tossed the pancake turner into the sink and disappeared around the corner.

Lucy heard him open the sliding glass door in the living room. Through the kitchen window she could see him out on the balcony, rummaging around the barbecue.

The strange moonlight bathed him in its eerie glow. Lucy felt compelled to speak his name. "Gil," she whispered. "My Gil."

He returned a minute later with a can of lighter fluid and matches. He doused the roaches and moved the pan to the center of the floor. He pulled a large match from the box.

Lucy cupped her hands around his. She took the match from his fingers and struck it off the side of the frying pan. "Turn off the light," she said.

Gilbert snapped the light off.

Lucy handed Gilbert the lighted match. He dropped it into the pan. The flames shot up a foot into the air.

They stood together at the window and watched the burning pyre, the blue and yellow flames dancing, their shadows dancing on the walls, the roaches dancing as their bodies crackled in the fire. Together they watched, sipping iced coffee, savoring the temporary salvation of humanity. What else could they do? ∎

Pillar Saint

ATOP A FIFTEEN meter pole, standing on a one-square-meter platform ringed by a baluster, tied to a stake to keep him upright, Simeon could see, when the winds were mild, a great ways off. Today there blew a low, cool, salty breeze, and the desert sand moved only in small ripples, like thousands of water snakes on the surface of a lake. He could see in the distance a brown dust cloud approaching. There came his mother's corpse, laid in the back of a cart, pulled by a single horse.

She came along the same route the bishop and elders had traveled when they arrived three decades ago to test his calling. They had stood that day at the base of his pillar and inquired whether he was motivated by piety or pride. Only one year earlier, he had been asked to leave the monastery. His extreme acts of penance and privation frightened and intimidated the other monks. In his year as a hermit, he had been on the move almost constantly from the crowds of supplicants and gawkers who had followed him into the wilderness and set up a small camp nearby.

"Brother Simeon," the bishop had asked, "what is the nature of your vocation?"

"Excellency, it is a call to purity," he replied, "to deep penance."

"And why does not a humble cell suffice? It served St. Anthony well."

"Although I cannot compare with the great father of hermits, I find myself in a dilemma that St. Anthony also faced. Pursued by disciples, heckled by enemies, jeered at by wayward children, I could find no solitude on earth, and so," he motioned with open hands to indicate his presence atop the pillar, "with much help, I chose to be suspended between heaven and earth."

Simeon thought he saw a sympathetic grin upon the bishop's lips but in the glare of the midday sun he could not be sure. The bishop and the elders interviewed some of the pilgrims who sought guidance from Simeon.

For there were many in the region who had exhausted their own spiritual resources and come to invoke his. They also interviewed the local boys who daily raised one bucket of flat bread and goat's milk and received down another bucket containing Simeon's meager waste. Then the holy men convened, prayed, took some tea, and re-approached Simeon's pillar.

The bishop announced sternly, "Simeon Stylites, you have made a shameful spectacle of yourself. Come down."

Shocked, confused, wounded, Simeon gripped the balustrade tightly. He looked heavenward. A large bird circled overhead. A vulture? He squinted as the vast wings crossed in front of the sun. "You see," whispered a tormenting spirit in his ear, "they have discovered your duplicity. The rank odor of your hypocrisy has soured their nostrils. Now all will know that your faith is mere chicanery." The voice was like a sharp stone scraping across an iron shield. "Descend," hissed the voice, "descend."

Glancing down at his hands, he saw that the blood had drained from his knuckles. The words of the psalmist came to mind: "My heart is in anguish within me, the terrors of death have fallen upon me. Fear and trembling come upon me, and horror overwhelms me." Defeated, he loosened his grip. Perhaps it had been pride after all, only pride that caused him to set himself apart. He would return home in utter shame. "O that I had wings like a dove! I would fly away and be at rest; truly, I would flee far away; I would lodge in the wilderness; I would hurry to find a shelter for myself from the raging wind and tempest." He looked down at the esteemed party. "I will obey," he finally said, hearing his own voice toll like a cracked, distant bell. He began to unfasten the leather strap that tethered his body to the stake.

Once the bishop and the elders saw that Simeon was willing to descend his perch, they rescinded the order. "Stay," the bishop called up. "You must remain faithful to your vocation. You do so with the blessing of Mother Church." He made the sign of the cross. "Simeon Stylites, may your words be as cool, flowing water, and may your presence be an oasis in this wilderness." The bishop and his entourage departed, satisfied that Simeon's motives were pure, that he still saw himself in alignment with his vows, that at least he could do no harm from such a height, and that at best he might in fact serve as an exemplar for the penitential life. As the brown cloud of dust arose in the wake of his departing, the bishop's words rang in Simeon's ears: Your words cool, flowing water. An oasis in the wilderness. And then the other voice contradicting: The rank odor of hypocrisy. Descend, descend.

For thirty years now he had waged war atop his pillar — praying, teaching, speaking with all who approached him, despite the doubts, the regrets, and despite the yearning of his legs to stand upon the firm earth again instead of constantly bracing against the wavering pillar as it listed in the wind. Simeon wrote letters, advised priests, princes, and peasants. He endured taunts, the hot sirocco, and intense loneliness. He was bone-thin, wrinkled, leathery, and radiant.

He had been joined one morning by a decrepit raven, who encircled him six times and lighted upon his baluster, then hopped to his arm, and perched finally on his shoulder. Thereafter, the bird assailed him daily, sitting on the sage's shoulder, cawing out across the desert wilderness. He did not lift his hand against it; rather, he accepted it as a kind of holy scourge, his thorn in the side. Simeon steeled himself against its repulsive manner: "But I call upon God, and the Lord will save me. Evening and morning and at noon I utter my complaint and moan, and he will hear my voice. He will redeem me unharmed from the battle that I wage, for many are arrayed against me."

Simeon shielded his eyes as he watched the brown cloud turned up by his mother's plain wooden hearse approach. And for the first time in many years, he felt the sting of tears roll from his eyes. The cart rocked to a stop at the base of his pillar and, as the dust cloud settled and the tarpaulin was removed from the cart, the whiteness of his mother's shroud was revealed. The raven alighted on the edge of the cart. With all his heart he wished he had a rock to heave at the foul scavenger.

The driver looked up toward Simeon and bowed awkwardly. This man had come to him some years ago to ask for Simeon's intercession on behalf of his sick wife. "Brother Simeon, you have blessed me with your strong prayers. My wife is restored to me. And so I asked if I might be the one to deliver your mother to you . . . as a token of my gratitude."

"I am glad to hear your wife is well."

"She is more than well. She nags and heckles me each and every day and beats me when she can catch me."

"I will pray that God restrain her spirit and bring you some peace."

"I had enough peace when she lay dying. Let her rail against me as she may. I prefer a lively, nagging wife to a sick, silent one."

"Has she given you any children?"

"Two boys. The youngest wants to be a priest. But Brother Simeon, I came not to speak of these things. I have the sad privilege of presenting to you the body of your dear mother. She died peacefully, as the other virgins stood vigil about her. They released her body to me yesterday. She smells of holly and lemon balm, sage and periwinkle. The virgins have warned me not to leave her body in the midday sun for long. She is to be buried in the nunnery garden at sunrise tomorrow."

"Thank you for bringing her to me." The stinging of his tears caused him to blink excessively. He welcomed the pain as an old friend. He had suffered much in his joints and in his limbs, as well as in his stomach. He had relished the pain in remembrance of the Lord's passion, as his small contribution to the redemption of mankind through penitential suffering. But the depth of grief that now overcame him was a new sort of pain. He felt it course through his entire body, from neck to chest, to groin, to knees and feet. The stinging sensation rang like a bell through his nervous system and he felt himself lurch forward at the sight of the man unwinding the shroud, exposing the head of his mother.

The voice of the raven spoke in his mind: "Your mother, too, was a failure and an impostor. Instead of praying for the sisters in her charge, she loitered in her precious garden, humming nonsense to the worms. And now those worms will devour her bit by bit." In his thoughts, Simeon countered the voice of the raven with the voice of the psalmist: "O God, you are my God, I seek you, my soul thirsts for you; my flesh faints for you, as in a dry and weary land where there is no water."

His mother had been his rock—friend, advisor, confessor. In the years before he had taken his vows, they had lived together in the city until the noise, vice, and nuisance of getting and spending began to smother their devotion. When Simeon received the call to the monastery, his mother went to live with the virgins, first as their gardener, cook, and maid, and eventually as holy sister and many years later, reverend mother.

After three decades atop his pillar, Simeon's body had grown stiff and dry as salted meat in his gradual mortification of it. Soon, he thought, it would cease to serve his spirit altogether and it would drop one day, as his mother's body had, among the herbs of her beloved garden in the home of the virgins. Just where, he wondered, would his body fall? Would he slump over one day like a spent animal, here, atop his pillar, his leather thong holding him in place? How long would it take the crowd under the canvas to realize he was dead, not just praying? A vision flashed into his mind of vultures pecking at his eyes, pulling his hair from the roots, tearing at the skin about his head and neck. Or would he sink into a soft bed somewhere, down there, on the ground again, in the home of the cart driver perhaps, or in the straw bunk of the parish priest who came four times a year to hear his confession and share the Eucharist?

For two days and nights since he had been told of her death, Simeon had imagined his mother wrapped in a shroud, according to custom. He had prepared himself to be confronted by its aroma, its whiteness, its finality. Yet somehow he had not prepared himself for the wave of emotion that would break over him when her face was revealed and he gazed upon her features, now lifeless and leaden. As the driver unwrapped his mother's head and lay it on a pillow he brought for the occasion, Simeon felt his breath stolen from his lungs and heard, as if from a great distance, a cry go up like the sudden pitch of an animal in the night. It was his own voice, of course. He had untied his leather harness in his grief and now felt himself leaning over the small rail of his baluster, reaching out with one hand toward his mother's body and holding the rail with the other. The heaving sobs that emerged were grotesque and selfish, distinctly unholy.

The driver joined a silent and awestruck throng of supplicants who stood beneath their canopy next to a small spring some ways from Simeon. In the decades of Simeon's ministry, this small camp had been pitched and maintained by the regulars for the comfort of those who traveled long distances to seek the prayers and guidance of the sage. They huddled now, trying in vain to divert their eyes from the spectacle of Simeon as he wailed, wept, and moaned.

For a moment Simeon thought he would abandon his calling. Why not surrender? He had stood watch here long enough. What had he accomplished, after all? He was a mere curiosity, the mad hermit of the Syrian desert. Why not admit it and be finished? He was merely a stubborn old monk who might now just as well bow to the elements. There would never be a better time. He wanted desperately to hold his mother again, to cradle her in his arms as she had so often cradled him in sickness or childhood fear. In his mind he heard himself call for the boys to bring the ladder. Yet his body continued to stand like a reed in the rising wind. He stared off into the distance.

The raven lighted on the hand that gripped the rail. The raven pecked at him, as if feeding upon the wrinkled skin on the back of his hand. Instinctively, he loosened his grip. The great black bird hopped up his arm and rubbed its beak in the folds of his tunic. "Look closely at her," the raven spoke. "All her prayers rose and fell to the dust, unheard and unheeded, just as yours. And now her body begins to rot and the flesh to melt from her bones. Soon yours," the raven lisped. "You should have spent your life in pleasure while you had the chance. You might as well descend. Perhaps there is still time to taste—"

The psalmist in his mind blocked out the voice of his tormentor: "Let the righteous rejoice in the Lord and take refuge in Him. Let all the upright in heart glory." Upon looking back at his mother's body, he realized there was no need for him to descend his perch. Below lay only her body, the shell that her soul had once animated. Her soul was now at peace in the bosom of the Lord. At this thought, his sentimental attachment to his mother's face subsided and so, slowly, did his tears. Soon he leaned back and stared at her in silence, turning his attention to the slow movement of his breath, as he had trained himself to do these many years. Then he stood upright, wiped his face, reattached his leather harness, and said a prayer for his mother's soul. It wasn't long before the driver apologetically re-wrapped his mother's head, covered her shroud with the tarpaulin, and drove slowly away.

As he watched the cart grow smaller and the dust cloud lift around the wheels of the cart, swirling and trailing, billowing and settling in her wake, he understood that he would never descend from his pillar. Here would be the place of his final breath when the time came. "Blessed be God, because he has not rejected my prayer or removed his steadfast love from me."

A dry, harsh sirocco began to blow in from the east. He lifted the edge of his tunic, tucked his chin, and sank into the posture that had become his only weapon against the extremities of the desert wilderness. The raven lifted from his shoulder, encircled him six times, and screeched as he flew west, chasing the quickly dropping sun as it made its way toward the ocean.

Simeon unfastened his leather harness, grabbed hold of his stake, and began a new form of devotion: as he prayed, reciting the names of the holy family so that they might be heard by those huddled beneath the canopy, he bowed deeply, touching his forehead to his knees. Up he rose, inhaling mightily, stretching as tall as he could. There he paused. Exhaling slowly, bending at the waist, down he bowed. A boy under the canopy watched in amazement and began to keep count, as the saint breathed and bowed and prayed. Even as the hot wind tugged at his frayed tunic, and even as darkness began to sweep across the desert, he could still see a great ways off. Simeon felt as though he were gliding, suspended somewhere between heaven and earth. ∎

The Art of Divination

At a gas station near a major freeway onramp, a father and his daughter park at adjacent pumps. They place the nozzles into their respective tanks and wait while the gas flows. He takes a squeegee from the bin next to the pump and cleans the windshield of his dingy gray-blue SUV; she sits in the front seat of her shiny red sports coupe, texting.

The daughter begins to sob. Staring at her phone, her free hand goes to her mouth. Her shoulders heave as her thumbs work the keypad. She hits the send button. Awaiting the reply, she sits still and stifles her tears. The people standing nearby try to look away. They feign disinterest by fiddling with the pumps and searching through their wallets.

Squeegee in hand, the father approaches her car, dragging a bum left leg. "What now?" he demands.

"Leave me alone," she says, wiping her cheeks.

"Get a hold of yourself." He wets the squeegee and begins washing her clean rear window.

The answer appears on her cell phone. She lets out a wail. She grasps her steering wheel with both hands in a feeble attempt to steady herself. Now the people at the other pumps abandon their attempts at polite disinterest. One lady approaches the daughter's car and asks, "Honey, are you all right?"

The father waves her off. "She's fine," he says. He turns to the daughter and hisses, "Give me that goddamned phone."

"Shut up," she says. "You don't know what I'm living through." She tries to type but gives up in frustration, looking to the sky. She sets her phone on the dash and pounds the steering wheel with the flat of her free hand.

"Sweetheart, you didn't invent bad love. Your generation didn't just discover crappy relationships that will never work."

She looks at him as though she is about to spit. "What do you know about love?"

Muscles flex in the father's jaw. He looks at the people who are staring at them and holds his baseball cap down as if a great wind tears at only him. The gas nozzle in his SUV clicks loudly as the pump turns off. He hobbles over and tries to replace the nozzle in its cradle. It takes a moment for him to realize that the task is harder with the squeegee in his hand. He looks at it as if it were a strange artifact he has just pulled from the earth. He sets it atop the pump and finishes his task. The pump beeps loudly. He takes a step back and stares, trying to figure out what the pump wants from him. When he tears his receipt from the machine, it finally falls silent.

The daughter climbs out of her car. "I can't go with you."

"What do you mean you can't go? You have to go."

"Look," she says, "just get on 280 right here and take it to 17. Go on over the hill. We've done this dozens of times together. You know the way. When you get to Highway 1, take a right near my school, that's north —"

"I can't do it," he interrupts. "I don't know where I'm going. The signs don't mean anything unless you're there. I need you to guide me so I don't get lost. That's what this whole thing is about, remember? I don't . . . I can't . . . ."

The gas nozzle in her car leaps as the pump clicks loudly off and makes them both jump. The daughter puts her hand over her heart.

"I have to go to Daniel."

"Daniel is over. Daniel is what's wrong with your life."

She points at her father. "You're what's wrong with my life." She curls her hair behind her ears. "I fucking hate you."

"Don't say that to me."

"You can't make me do this. I have to go to Daniel."

"Did you forget I've got this thing . . . this thing in my . . . ?" He searches for the words and can't find them. He smacks the right side of his head. "Did you forget what the fucking Iraqis did to me?"

"Everybody knows what the fucking Iraqis did to you. What they don't know is what you did to you." She yanks the nozzle from her tank and replaces it on its cradle.

He tugs at his goatee and speaks deliberately. "Listen to me now. Daniel doesn't love you. Isn't that what he's telling you on your . . . your . . . ."

"It's called a phone."

"Forget about Daniel. He's last week's garbage."

"You don't know what you're talking about."

"I'm damaged, yes," the father says. "But look at my eyes. Look how clear they are. Not a drink in sixteen months — not a toke, not a drink, not a snort." His torso strains towards her as if he's leaning into a wave. "I'm clean in body, mind, and spirit."

The daughter slouches against her car and sighs. She rests the back of her head on the top of the driver's side door. Against gunmetal clouds, a flock of geese fly in perfect V formation, honking directions to anyone who might be listening. When the pump begins to beep at her, she reaches over matter-of-factly and tears free her receipt. She looks at it as if the gas receipt holds the secret to her happiness. If she could just crack the code, all would be well.

Still staring at the gas receipt, she says, "You have no idea what I'm living through."

He tightens her gas cap until it clicks into place, then pushes the lid closed.

"I have to go to him," she says. "He needs me."

"I need you."

"I can't take this," she says to the gas pump. "You can't fucking do this to me."

"I'm your father," he says. He moves between his daughter and the pump, puts both of his hands on both of her shoulders and looks at her over the gas receipt. "I'm your father." He tries to gain eye contact. "I'm —"

Her cell phone rings. The bystanders are frozen in tableau. The phone rings and rings again. In awkward, jerky movements, the father grabs her cell phone and limps away. His bum left leg drags behind, scuffing the asphalt. The daughter reaches out to stop him. In the middle of the gas station, he raises the phone over his head and ceremoniously dashes it to the ground.

The father and the daughter stand over the silent mass of cell phone shards spread before them on the asphalt. In certain ancient Roman temples, priests examined the entrails of sheep in such a manner, believing the patterns made by the animal's intestines could shed light on their predicament.

No one has left the gas station, though their tanks are filled and their windshields are clean. They stand and stare at the father and the daughter. The daughter drops to her knees and begins picking up the pieces. The father watches her and then, sliding his bum leg out to the side, drops contritely to his good knee. He takes off his cap, revealing a jagged red scar above his right ear. He holds his cap out. She drops pieces of phone into the cap.

The gas station manager emerges from his office with a broom and dustpan. He slows and stops. Everyone watches her pick up every last piece, bit by bit, and drop them into her father's cap. ∎

Middle of Nowhere

THE BELL OVER the door clanged when the father walked into the coffee shop and sat in a booth next to the window. After he got himself settled, he lay a pack of cigarettes and a lighter out on the table in front of him. The son watched him from behind the counter, then walked back into the kitchen and spoke to the owner. "Can I take my break now?" he asked.

The owner peeked his head through the kitchen doorway and surveyed the tables.

There was a young couple at the counter involved in a flirtatious conversation. Their coffee cups were full. There was a man reading a book in one booth, a half-eaten donut on his plate. And there was a new customer who had just parked himself in another booth and was staring out the window. "Help him first," he said, nodding at the man.

The son approached the father and said, "They won't let you smoke in here."

The father looked directly at him for the first time since coming into the coffee shop.

The son said, "Let me get you a cup of coffee."

"I didn't come for coffee."

"I know," said the son, "but it'd be better for me if you'd let me set a cup in front of you." He went behind the counter and poured him a cup. He set it on the table next to the father's cigarettes and sat down opposite him in the booth.

"How'd you find me?" he asked.

"I hired a private detective," he said. "It didn't take him long to find you because you used your credit card to buy gas and your cell phone to call work. These things are easy to trace. He said if you were serious about disappearing you would've planned it better."

"I was serious about it," the son said, "just stupid. It didn't occur to me to trash the card and the phone until after I'd already used them. After I'd already laid down a trail. My only hope was that no one would be especially motivated to find me."

"If it was just me I might've let you go this time. You're not a teenager anymore, after all. But you didn't just run away from your parents this time. You left your wife and baby son. You left them without a car in an apartment with two months rent over their heads."

The father took a cigarette from his pack and stuck the filter in his lips. The son opened his mouth to begin to repeat the no-smoking rule but stopped himself. The father flicked his lighter and lit his cigarette. His eyes scanned the table for an ashtray. He took an empty saucer from the next table and set it in front of him.

"How long have you been working here?"

"A week."

The father turned to look out the window at the parking lot. "How's the car running?"

"Fine. It's a little sluggish going uphill."

"Why'd you choose this place?"

"I didn't really choose it. It's just where I stopped."

"Why'd you stop?"

"It seemed like a good place. I wanted to . . . think."

"Been thinking a lot, have you?"

"I'm not going back."

Blowing smoke and flicking the ashes from his cigarette, the father said, "You prefer this place to a wife who loves you and a baby who needs you?"

The son waved the cigarette smoke away from his face. "You wouldn't understand."

"Try me."

"I'm tired of explaining myself."

"You don't think you owe the people you've hurt an explanation? You really think you can just get up and leave anytime you want?"

"I can't talk to you about this."

"Why?"

"Because I don't think that way. I don't think the way you do."

"Tell me how you think."

"I'm not going back."

"So you said."

"I'm not sixteen anymore. You can't put me in the car and take me home."

"Do you realize what you just said? You're not sixteen. But you're still acting like you're sixteen. Still running. It's time for you to grow up."

"You can't do this. You can't just come in here and take me back. I'm an adult. I can do what I want."

"Because you can doesn't mean you should."

"No more shoulds for me. From now on I do what I want."

"What do you want? I'm guessing your heart's desire doesn't include serving coffee in a crappy diner in the middle of nowhere."

"I'm out of money, which you already know if you hired a detective."

"Why is it better for you to be out of money here than at home, surrounded by your wife and child?"

"I'm not like you."

"So you said." He flicked the ashes from his cigarette. He took a sip from the coffee cup. "Where's the restroom?"

The son hooked his thumb over his shoulder. The father balanced his cigarette on the edge of the saucer and walked back to the restroom. His entire childhood the son watched ashes fall from the father's cigarettes. He felt as if he had spent years on end coughing and waving smoke away from his face. The dog they had when he was younger would often sit beside the father's chair and lap at the father's cigarette smoke with his tongue. In some ways that dog had been the son the father never had.

The owner came out from the kitchen. "What's going on?" he asked, leaning on the table.

"Just taking my break."

"Friend of yours?" he asked, nodding toward the restroom.

"I don't know him."

"Looks kind of like you. You with thirty years more living and a pair of glasses."

The owner took a pack of licorice chewing gum from his shirt pocket. He pulled out a piece and unwrapped it, popped it in his mouth. He dropped the rest of the pack on the table. "I'll give you a raise," he said, beginning to chew his stick of gum.

"I didn't ask for one."

"People don't just move to this town, like you did. They pass through. Usually they're on their way to Reno. Or they've been hired to work at the penitentiary over in Folsom. Or they've got a carload of backpacking gear and they're going to rough it in the wilderness for a week. You. You looked lost when you walked in here last week. I could've sworn you were going to ask me for directions."

"You had the 'now hiring' sign in the window."

"That sign's been up for four years." He worked the gum around in his mouth. "I'll give you a dollar more an hour if you stay. I can afford more later."

"Why?"

"You're a nice kid. You don't bother the regulars. Just bring them their coffee and stand back. They like that."

"I'm not a kid."

"Right. I meant compared to me. If somebody's going to fill your coffee cup it's better he's not a grizzled old poop, like me."

The son looked over his shoulder toward the restroom.

"Offer's on the table," the owner said, as he ambled back behind the counter. He grabbed a rag, wet it in the sink, and began wiping down the countertop.

The father emerged from the restroom and returned to his seat opposite the son. He flicked the ashes from his cigarette onto the saucer and returned the filter to his lips.

He picked up the pack of gum and pretended to read its label. "Tell me what you think it is about me that's so different from you."

"Everything."

"We may be more alike than you know." He took a long drag on his cigarette and blew the smoke up over their heads.

The owner retreated back into the kitchen. They could hear the sound of water running and dishes clanking. The couple at the counter twittered like a pair of birds in a cage. Giggling, the girl kept slapping the boy on his shoulder, and he kept rubbing his shoulder, pretending that it hurt. The man in the other booth closed his book, finished his donut, and left. The bell over the door clanged as he shuffled across the parking lot. As the door slowly closed behind him, the sound of cars on the highway was like the sound of a distant waterfall.

It became clear to the son that the father would not leave until he had heard what he came to hear — a reason, an explanation. The son felt the owner looking at him from the kitchen. Well, he had a ten-minute break and he would finish it, then get up and go back to work. If the father wanted to sit all evening in the booth, that was his business. He would give the father his break. Maybe he owed him that much.

"You're this beacon of responsibility," he said to the father. "You've never had any doubts about the way you live. You do everything right. You got your job as a salesman. You worked your way up to management. You got married. You had children. You bought a house in the suburbs. You voted Republican. You took us all to church on Sundays. As far as I can see, you've never wavered from your devotion to us. When I ran away, you came and brought me home. You're still doing it."

"Why do you keep running away?"

The son shook his head and raised his hands as if befuddled. "I . . . want to be free. I don't . . . want to be tied down. I don't know how to say it. I don't want to have to be responsible for other people." He held his hands up. "I know what you're going to say: too late."

"Looks to me like you've succeeded. You've run away from your family and your job. You're free right now. You're living your dream. You're living exactly the life you've chosen for yourself. Except that your ass really belongs to that guy in the kitchen, right? When this coffee break ends, you're back to working for him. So why is it better to work for him than to work for people who love you?"

"I'm not talking about love."

The father twisted his cigarette on the edge of the saucer, using its rim to carve the tip of ashes into a glowing point. He took a deep drag. "You're right about one thing," he said. "I've never just taken off, like you have. But that doesn't mean I haven't wanted to. Where you're wrong is in saying I never wanted to. Everybody wavers. Everybody has doubts about the choices they've made and regrets about the life they've lived. The only difference between us is that I counted the cost of leaving and found it too expensive. I'm talking now about the emotional cost. Look — the longer you stay out here the harder your heart will become, until someday you won't be able to come back. You've seen those guys with weathered faces and that distant, vague look in their eyes, like an animal keen only on survival. They're all dried up inside. If you stay out here, that's your destination. If you come home, you'll at least have a chance for something else."

"What if that something else turns out to be a kind of slavery?"

"Look around you. If this doesn't look like slavery to you, then stay. I'm not here to bring you home again. This is your decision. You'll have to bring yourself home."

The son looked out the window at the parking lot. The father had pulled his Audi right up to the front bumper of the son's Chevrolet. The two cars were facing each other just as the father and the son now faced each other in the booth.

The father put his cigarette out in the saucer. He pulled some money from his wallet and tucked it beneath the pack of cigarettes. The son couldn't bring himself to look the father in the eyes. Instead, he focused on the cars out in the parking lot. He wondered how much daylight was left, how much time before the lights over his car would pop on, signaling the end of his shift, give or take a few minutes.

"I hope I'll see you again," the father said. He stood and walked out of the coffee shop. The son watched as the father got into his Audi and slowly drove away. He looked down at the table. There lay the pack of gum and the pack of cigarettes. Sticking out from beneath the cigarettes was a $100 bill. He scooped up the money and the cigarettes, leaving the gum on the table.

He walked out into the parking lot and stood looking westward. The sky overhead was a deep blue but the clouds on the horizon were orange and pink. The air up at this altitude was fresh and pine-scented. He put one of the father's cigarettes into his mouth and lit it. The smoke made him squint, and it burned all the way down his throat and into his lungs. He looked down at the cigarette between his thumb and index finger. He flicked the ashes to the asphalt and raised the cigarette again to his lips.

The owner of the coffee shop stood with hands on hips inside the window at the booth where the son had sat with the father a few moments earlier. Suddenly the light over his car flickered and stayed on. He glanced at his wristwatch. Every evening this week the light had popped on at closing time. That was still two hours away.

If he started driving now, he could be home before morning. If he left right now, in fact, he could gas up the car and catch up to the father, following in his wake. He imagined the way the father's Audi would hug the curves all the way down the mountain. He had a pretty clear picture of what his life would look like if he did that. He dropped the cigarette and stepped on it. It was harder to picture the other life, the one he'd have if he stayed out here, in the middle of nowhere, with $100 as seed money. It would start with serving coffee at a cheap diner off exit 162 of a mountain highway, but there was no way of knowing where things would go from there. ∎

Like You Don't Really Care

WE WERE SITTING on the front stoop of Jim's apartment in the late afternoon of a hot midsummer's day. Jim's parents were inside fighting. We could hear their voices coming from the back bedroom. My parents had never sounded like that. Don't get me wrong, my parents argued now and then. But my parents didn't have that tone in their voices that bespoke pure hatred. In fact, I'd never heard that tone anywhere else except from actors on television. It frightened and fascinated me. What could people possibly do or say to each other to result in such utter despair?

Around lunchtime, Jim and I had ridden our bikes to the park and fished in the lake. We weren't very hungry, so we used most of the hot dogs we had taken from Jim's fridge as bait. We didn't catch anything, but then we hadn't expected to. If there were fish in the lake, we knew they would all be resting on the bottom in the middle of the day. It was just something to do. For me, a summer's day opened up before me with an expansiveness I could not imagine filling. Fishing when there was no possibility of catching fish seemed as good a pastime as any when all you had was time. I didn't understand then that, for Jim, our simple trip to the park was a welcome escape from the circle of hell his parents had created for him.

And now we were sucking Popsicles on Jim's front stoop. But the Popsicles were melting faster than we could eat them, and our hands were stained with the sticky red juice as it dripped all the way down our skinny forearms. Deep inside the apartment, Jim's parents were yelling things I'd never heard before.

"I wish the firemen would come around today and open up the hydrants," Jim said.

After a minute of thought, I said, "We could turn on the garden hose again."

"It's not the same," Jim immediately answered.

He was right, of course. Squirting each other with the hose was not as good as the excitement of all the neighborhood kids when the huge truck rolled up; not nearly as good as the big firemen in their yellow coats and red helmets, turning the spout with a giant wrench; and no way as good as the rush of cold water that nearly knocked us over with its power, momentarily flooding our street.

Jim's sister opened the screen door and slipped outside, making sure to shut the screen quietly behind her.

"Is he leaving again?" Jim asked.

"Looks like it," she answered. "He's trying to pack a bag and she keeps unpacking it."

She too had a Popsicle in her hand and sat beside us, looking out at the empty street. There was a kind of weary, resigned tone in her voice. I knew from previous conversations that Jim's dad wasn't his real dad. But he was Jim's sister's real dad. And Jim's mom was not Jim's sister's real mom. But she was Jim's. At my house, both my mom and dad were mine and my sister's real parents. This situation at Jim's house was a kind of curiosity to me. What would I do if I needed to talk to my dad, but he wasn't my dad?

We heard a crash inside the apartment. I looked at Jim. I looked at his sister. They were both looking out at the street. And then we heard a door slam. I stood up. That was enough for me. I didn't want to be around anymore.

"Sit down," Jim told me.

"Do you think you should call somebody?" I asked.

"Who?"

I sat down. I couldn't say out loud how afraid I was. I could have run away, but the shame I would feel afterwards would be hard to live with. But something told me that I wasn't safe. That something awful could happen at any moment. That instead of grown-ups being calm and polite and controlled, they could also be wild and vicious and dangerous. They could do things to themselves and to children that could not be undone.

I stood again. Someone was coming. It was Jim's father who appeared at the door.

Or rather Jim's sister's father. I wanted to run but my feet were stuck to the porch. Suddenly my mouth went completely dry. Jim's sister's father was standing on the other side of the screen door, slipping his arms into a sportcoat. A sportcoat when it was ninety degrees out.

He pushed open the screen door and set his suitcase on the stoop. He flicked his cigarette over onto the front lawn. He had two thin red stripes down one cheek. Fresh cuts. "Well," he said. He stood there looking out at the street. It was one of those days when the heat waves billow up off the asphalt, and if you squinted your eyes you could easily imagine some sort of mirage. I'd seen a movie about a pair of misfits who joined the foreign legion. They ended up in a desert far from home, dying of thirst. Everywhere they trudged they saw an oasis. They kept diving into the sand, thinking they were diving into a cool pool of water shaded by palm trees.

Jim flicked his Popsicle stick onto the lawn. Jim's sister threw hers there too, even though she had half of her Popsicle left. Inside the house we heard Jim's mother sobbing. Her voice sounded both sleepy and angry. She had been begging her husband to stay.

Jim's sister's father picked up his suitcase and slipped between us almost apologetically, the way people do when they say "Excuse me," but he didn't say anything. He put his suitcase into the trunk of the beat up Plymouth Road Runner parked at the curb. The television slogan ran through my mind: "And the Plymouth win-you-over beat goes on!" He ran his fingers through his hair and looked on down the street. He shook the car keys in his hand the way gamblers on television do with dice. He turned toward us like he wanted to say something. I couldn't imagine what would come out of his mouth. And I guess he couldn't either because nothing did. He got into his car, started it up, and drove away. All three of us watched his Plymouth go down the street.

Jim's mom opened the screen door. She'd been standing inside watching him go.

She had two black stripes of mascara running down her cheeks, and the sleeve of her blouse was torn off her shoulder, exposing her bra strap.

"Is he coming back this time?" Jim asked.

"I can't say. This might be it. This might be it for good." She sucked in air quickly and let it out in little wisps. I'd never seen anybody cry like that. Like she was starting to blow up a balloon that was hard to get going. We were all of us staring down the street in the direction he had driven, but we couldn't see the car anymore.

"Don't come in the house for a little while, kids," she said. "I need some time alone. And then I need to clean up a bit. And then I need to call Aunt Tillie." She went back inside. A half-minute later she came back out with a handwritten note and a five dollar bill. She handed these to Jim's sister. "Run down to the corner store and get me a carton of cigarettes," she told her.

Jim's sister took the five and the note addressed to the store owner that gave her permission to buy the cigarettes. "I thought you quit," she said.

"I did. Seems like a good day to start up again." She ran her fingers across Jim's sister's bangs. "I hope you won't hold it against me."

After Jim's sister got a ways down the block, Jim said to his mother, "Will he come back for her?"

"She's ours now," his mother said. She looked down at us. "Why don't you boys go on a bike ride? Beautiful day like this, I don't know why you want to sit around. Boys ought to be on the move. It isn't natural to sit around like you do."

"I don't want to go back to the trailer park," Jim said. "Aunt Tillie's perfume is putrid. It makes me sick."

"So noted," his mother said. She went back inside. Something else broke in there, I don't know what. A vase maybe. And then we heard some cupboards slamming.

Jim stood up, finally, and ran his fingers through his hair. "It's cooled down a bit," Jim said. "Let's take our fishing poles back to the lake. There might be some shadows around the shoreline near the baseball field."

"I'm beginning to wonder if there are any fish in there at all," I said.

"Of course there's fish in there. Cam Johnson pulled a twelve-inch catfish out of the lake last week."

"I don't know if we can believe Cam Johnson," I said. "Anyway, I'm pretty sure my mom said something about being home this afternoon. I may have a dentist's appointment or something."

Jim looked at me and tried to smile. Something caught in his throat. He coughed and turned to spit while he threw his leg over the seat of his bike. We both knew I was abandoning him, leaving him like his father had, or rather his sister's father had. "See you," he said as he rode off slowly in the direction of the park.

"Yeah, see you," I said. I thought about yelling after him that he forgot his fishing pole. But then I realized he wasn't going fishing. He didn't care about fish anymore than I did. He rode off slowly, making S-shaped curves on his Stingray, going up on the sidewalk, then out into the street, then up onto the sidewalk again. Like that. Like when you're on your way somewhere, but not really. Like you don't really care when, or if, you get there. ▪

Inheriting the Earth

IT WAS AFTER school on a cloudy but unusually warm Monday in early November. Bret had eaten his snack and was walking up the sidewalk on his way to the park. He had an hour before homework time and his favorite afternoon TV program had been canceled due to tomorrow's national election. Nixon and McGovern weren't exactly neck and neck according to the polls; nevertheless, the afternoon variety shows had been preempted so that the news anchors could talk and talk about the issues. He had trouble understanding how the grown-ups could maintain their interest in so much talk. His teacher had told him to watch the news special about the election at eight o'clock tonight and jot three ideas to discuss in school the next morning.

The entire school was holding a mock election: the morning would be devoted to classroom caucuses, with speeches by the older kids during lunch hour, followed by voting in the afternoon. Class officers would stay after school to tally the votes; they would announce the results on Wednesday morning right along with the national results. Bret knew his father was for Nixon and his mother was for McGovern, but really he couldn't see what all the fuss was about. The war was on in Vietnam, and he knew that McGovern was against it. That seemed like a good idea. Bret wondered why his dad wouldn't want the war to end.

Two men were planting new trees along the parkway next to the sidewalk. Three holes had been dug into the damp grass. One man was balancing the trunk of a young tree on his shoulder while the other was cutting away the burlap sack around the root ball. Their pick up truck was parked at the curb with two other young trees in the bed. The windows on the truck were down and Jim Morrison was singing on the radio. A boy about Bret's age, maybe a year younger, stood by watching them. He was shorter than Bret, stockier, with shaggy blonde hair that hadn't been washed or combed in a while.

The man holding the tree looked at Bret as he approached. It made Bret uncomfortable, though he didn't know why. There was something strange about him, and the man's eyes were scanning up and down. As Bret got closer, the man got his partner's attention. "Look at this guy. He looks like a tough guy."

The man cutting the burlap with his pocketknife looked at Bret and smiled. "Yeah, he's a tough guy, all right. Don't be fooled by them skinny arms and buck teeth."

They laughed. "Hey Tony," the one balancing the tree said to the boy. "You think you can take this guy?"

The boy looked at Bret and shrugged. Bret had slowed down to watch the men work. He stopped now, next to them on the sidewalk, as the boy, Tony, looked him over. The man with the pocketknife motioned to Tony. "Stand over there, Tony Boy," he said. Bret got the impression that Tony was the man's son, and that Tony was working with his dad and his partner today, or at least tagging along on this job. "Stand right there next to the tough guy." He was wearing a camouflage shirt, like the soldiers Bret had seen on the evening news. It was part of the uniform they wore in the jungles of Vietnam. The organ playing along with Jim Morrison reminded him of the one in church, but distorted a bit, more like the organ music in horror movies.

A voice in Bret's head told him to keep moving down the sidewalk. But another voice told him to stand firm. What would his dad want him to do? He was supposed to listen to adults when they spoke to him and show them respect. These men didn't look anything like his dad. Their clothes were dirty and torn. They were listening to rock 'n' roll on the radio, not The Ames Brothers or The Lettermen. The man holding the tree was missing some teeth and looked to Bret a bit like a TV pirate. He wore a bandanna around his head, had a gold earring in his ear, and a pack of Marlboro's stuffed into the rolled up sleeve of his T-shirt. "You can take him, can't you Tony?" said the man with the earring.

Tony shrugged again and looked at the ground. His father tossed his pocketknife into the grass next to Bret's tennis shoe where it stuck deep in the softened soil. His father clapped Tony's shoulder. "Abso-fucking-lutely he could take him. This guy's a chump, Tony Boy. You could drop him in two punches."

Tony looked up at Bret now. Bret thought he had an embarrassed look on his face. "Tony's got fists like hammers," the pirate man said. Jim Morrison's voice now imitated the distorted organ music. He imagined this was what Peter Lorre might sound like if he could sing, like he was strangling an animal while crooning at the window of a lover.

Again Bret felt the impulse to move, maybe even to run. These men had the bodies and the deep voices of grown-ups, but he had never known a grown-up to encourage fighting among boys. He had seen a movie on television about a bull terrier whose owner entered him in dogfights. These men behaved like the dog's owner in the movie, sizing up other boys to fight their boy. Bret had been in playground scraps before, with other boys his age who, like pups, wanted to show who was top dog. But this situation was confusing all around. These grown ups not only didn't oppose fighting, they seemed to be excited by the prospect of pitting their Tony against him.

Tony's father stood too close to Bret, plucked his knife up from the grass, wiped the mud from the blade on his bell-bottom jeans, folded it closed, and tucked it into his hip pocket. Bret thought if he tried to run now, they would stop him. "Let me see your fists," the father said. "Put 'em up, chump." Bret heard himself laugh at the funny rhyme the father had made, like something out of a cartoon, but he knew right away that his laugh had insulted the father. Muscles in the man's jaw tightened. Stupid nervous laugh. Should he apologize? "Fists," the father said.

Bret looked down at his hands. He curled his fingers into fists and held them awkwardly at his waist. The pirate man said to Tony, "Put 'em up, Big T. Show this skinny fucker your equipment."

Bret opened his fists and took a step backward. He checked the faces of the two grown men to see if they were maybe joking. They were smiling at him, yes, but it was the kind of smile Edward G. Robinson wore in the

Warner Brothers gangster movies Bret watched on TV Saturday afternoons. It was the smile he smiled when he had a gun in his hand and some poor sap in a corner pleading for his life. On the truck radio, the distorted organ music had overcome Jim Morrison now and all Bret could hear was Morrison grunting along with the drawn-out notes.

Tony took a step forward and pushed Bret. Bret stumbled backward and tripped on a sprinkler head. He was sitting on the grass now with Tony standing over him, fists cocked. Tony looked at his father, who spoke approvingly. "That's the stance," he said. "Keep your left up and fire from the shoulder." The pirate man dropped the tree he had been holding and circled around to get a clearer view. The three of them waited for Bret to stand.

Bret wasn't sure if he should stand or stay down. It seemed like all three of them — the two grown-ups and Tony — were going to fight him now. Why? What had he done to them? Bret thought this might be an episode of *Candid Camera*, but they were in an open area with no place to hide a television camera.

Bret tried to figure what his father would want him to do in this situation. His father had told him it was all right for him to defend himself. But the one time Bret had actually gotten into a real fight, not just a playground tussle, his father said he was disappointed in him, that he should have walked away. In Sunday School a few weeks later the lesson had been about turning the other cheek. Everyone knew the Sunday School teacher's son had been drafted to fight in Vietnam. A girl in the class had boldly raised her hand and asked if the teacher thought Jesus was talking about war. The teacher's ears turned red. "That's a very good question, Becky," she replied. "I'd say that's the $64,000 question."

Tony stood his ground, fists up, his jaw set. "Stand up and fight, you pussy," said the pirate man.

Bret stayed put. He had assumed that word was one only boys used to show off how tough they were to other boys. It sounded strange in the mouth of a grown-up, even a grown-up who looked like a pirate.

Tony's father kicked the bottom of Bret's tennis sneaker. "Get up and fight or we'll throw you in the back of the truck and take you for a ride."

"Let's take him down to the beach and see if he knows how to swim," said pirate man.

Bret pushed himself up and got to his feet but refused to lift his hands. Tony pushed him again, but Bret kept his footing. Tony gave his father an exasperated look. "What am I supposed to do if he won't fight?"

"He'll fight," said his father. "Spit on him."

Tony put his hands down and looked at his father. "You heard me," his father said, "spit in his goddamn face!"

Tony made that hawking noise in his throat like he was trying to gather saliva. But it was pirate man who launched a gob of spittle onto Bret's face. He felt himself flinch and blink. Then Tony's father spat on Bret, hitting his neck and shoulder. Tony tried to contribute but only sprayed a little saliva onto Bret's T-shirt. When Bret pulled up the edge of his T-shirt to wipe the spit from his eye, Tony threw his first punch, a right to Bret's stomach. And then Tony brought his left straight across Bret's jaw.

The pirate man laughed in delight. Tony's father said, "That's my Tony Boy!"

Bret took another step back.

"Ah, he's just a little pussy," said the pirate man. "Look, he's crying."

Bret wasn't crying. He just stood there, holding his jaw. It didn't hurt, not really; he'd just never been hit so squarely in the jaw before. He expected it to hurt more. He expected the punch to sound more like punches do in the movies. But there was hardly any sound. Whenever Elvis punched somebody in one of his movies, there was a loud smack and the guy went flying backwards.

"I think he shit his pants, Tony Boy," said his father. "Tough guy's standing like he's got a load in his Fruit of the Looms."

"You kicked his ass," said pirate man, raising Tony's arm to proclaim him winner. "Nice work, killer."

Tony's father grabbed Bret by the T-shirt and pulled him close. Bret could smell beer and peanuts on his breath. Out of the corner of his eye, Bret saw the pirate man moving to his left. "I'm glad you're not my kid," the father said. "If you were my son, I'd kill myself for shame. I feel sorry for your father to have such a poor excuse for a son." He pushed Bret backwards. Meantime, the pirate man had crept around behind Bret and stooped down. Bret fell hard over pirate man's back and flipped to one side, rolling back to land hard on the sidewalk. The two men laughed hilariously.

"Run to mama," said Tony's father.

Bret got to his feet and looked eye to eye with Tony. Was it just his imagination or did Tony have an apologetic look on his face? The pirate man picked up one of the shovels and took a threatening step in Bret's direction. Bret turned and walked away, peals of derisive laughter ringing in his ears. He picked up his pace to a jog. He looked over his shoulder and saw the two men still watching him, still laughing. Tony had taken up the tree and was planting it into the hole. After crossing the street at the corner, he ran the remaining two blocks to the park without looking back.

HE SAT IN one of the swings to catch his breath. He watched the street to see if the pick up truck would come after him. He wasn't sure what they were capable of. After his breathing evened out again, Bret leaned back in the swing and kicked with his sneakers in the sand to gently twirl himself around, tangling the chains that connected the heavy canvas swing to the overhead bar. He was watching the pale afternoon sunlight through the leaves of a tall maple, enjoying the way the dizziness came and went as he twirled, the chains tangling into a tight bunch over his head. When he lifted his feet from the ground, he spun quickly, jerking a bit from side to side, as the chains untangled and he slowed to a stop.

He was thinking about Tony and his dad and the pirate man. What sort of a man wore an earring in his ear? What kind of a life must Tony have with a father who demanded he fight with strangers? Bret's father was a businessman. He left the house early, before Bret was up for school, and he returned home at dark in his blue business suit, smelling of cigarette smoke and after-shave lotion. He lifted Bret and hugged him as he came through the door. Until this year he had carried Bret into the kitchen, where he greeted his wife and kissed her as she stirred their dinner on the stove.

Now Bret was growing too big to be carried so easily. Bret couldn't imagine what Tony's house was like, couldn't picture his mother, or the bed Tony slept in, or the toys he had, or the records he listened to.

You could learn a little about people from the movies, but clearly there were things in this world that no movie could dramatize. If Tony's dad was Edward G. Robinson, a man who took pleasure in other people's pain, then Bret's dad was Frederick March, a man who would never pick on others just for kicks, especially not kids. And the pirate man: he was part Elisha Cook, Jr. and part Jack Palance. But that didn't help much. There was no one to play him in the movies. You would have to pull him together from not only a pirate movie but a war movie and a gangster picture. He would have scars all over, like Frankenstein, from being cobbled together like that. And the scars would somehow fit him.

On occasion Bret would spar with his father, throw punches at his upheld palms like Anthony Quinn and Mickey Rooney in *Requiem for a Heavyweight*. Sometimes they would wrestle on the living room floor. Bret could tell that his father didn't really enjoy these sessions. He would play along for awhile, but when Bret would get too rambunctious, his father would say, "Take it easy, sport. We're just playing, remember?" But sometimes Bret had trouble controlling himself. His father was so much bigger than he was that Bret imagined whatever he did, he could never hurt him. In those moments when Bret got too rough and rowdy, his father would grab Bret's hands and press them together. The more Bret struggled to release his hands, the more his father's grip tightened, until, red in the face, Bret would relax his muscles. His father would quote from his favorite movie, *The Gunfighter*, a line that Gregory Peck spoke to a young outlaw who challenged him, "How come I've got to run into a squirt like you nearly every place I go these days?" This was his father's signal that rough play was over.

"Oh, come on!" Bret would beg.

His father would raise his hands high. "I'm a lover, not a fighter," he would say.

Some older boys Bret recognized from school were tossing a football over on the grass. Soon the tallest among them, a Hawaiian boy named

Ricky, approached Bret. They had five guys, he explained, not enough for even teams. Did Bret want to join them and make it three-against-three? The playing field would stretch from the edge of the basketball court all the way up to the sidewalk. The drinking fountain was out-of-bounds on the opposite side, and the edge of the sand here at the swings was out on this side. Bret nodded. "You'll be on my team," Ricky said.

It was a good game. Ricky and the other boys were good athletes. Bret had watched them from the corners of his own games on the playground at school. These boys were seventh- and eighth-graders, and at school they were not allowed to mix with the younger grades because of the size difference. The teachers did not want the younger boys to get hurt. Even though these older boys played hard and took the game seriously, they didn't pick on Bret or take advantage of his slender frame. In fact, because of his height, Bret was able to knock down a couple of opposing passes, nearly intercepting one of them. And because these boys were skilled at the game and more competitive than the younger boys Bret usually played with, he played better than usual. He ran just a bit faster, caught the ball just a bit more often, and blocked when a block was needed, not just when he felt like colliding with another boy.

At the drinking fountain after the game, the other boys asked Bret his name and if he came to the park often. They were there nearly every day during football season, but they had to leave by four-thirty because Ricky and another boy had to practice piano for an hour before dinner. Bret was welcome to join them. "By the way," Ricky said, "tell your folks to vote for Nixon tomorrow. My dad says that other guy is a Communist."

On the walk back home, Bret quizzed himself on the boys' names and wondered if it would be all right to call them by name when he saw them tomorrow at school. They might not want to acknowledge a younger boy among friends in their own grade level. He remembered seeing one of his sister's high school friends at the shopping mall and calling out hello to him. The older boy had ignored Bret. Bret's sister explained to him later that the boy did not want to acknowledge that he was friendly with a younger boy. It was a matter of honor, she explained. You could not be seen with "babies" if you wanted to keep your reputation.

HE HAD TEMPORARILY forgotten about Tony. But when he came to the stretch of sidewalk where the altercation had occurred, he stopped. The truck was gone. The new trees were all firmly planted in the parkway. The soil was tamped down; there was a ring of freshly-watered flowers around the base of each young tree. The only sign of violence was the scuffed spot in the grass near the sprinkler head where he had fallen when Tony pushed him. Bret had forgotten about it during the football game; he wondered if he could forget about it altogether, or if this would be one of the things that went through his mind over and over on nights when it was difficult to sleep.

Standing now in the spot where it happened, his stomach felt queasy, and he remembered Tony's punches, as if he could feel them again — one to the stomach and one to the jaw. It was less of a physical memory as an emotional one. He had not cried. But he had not fought back. Did this count as turning the other cheek? Had he dishonored himself?

He still wasn't sure what his father would have done in that situation. A young Frederick March would surely not have backed down after being spat upon. He remembered his father had justified the Vietnam war once by saying that the United States could not just stand there when provoked by the Communists. His father was reading the newspaper at the kitchen table. His mother had said, "If you're really strong, you don't need to fight," as she set a plate of eggs and toast before him. His father had returned her comment with a stern look.

"I suppose the South Koreans should have just welcomed the Communists into their country when they crossed the 38th parallel? And I suppose, instead of spending two years of our lives fighting them back, we should have just politely asked them to leave?"

Bret looked up from his oatmeal. He had not heard this tone between his father and mother before. His mother looked stunned. She began to open her mouth; it looked to Bret like she was going to apologize. Then it suddenly looked like she was going to cry. Then her face took on two or three different expressions, expressions Bret had not seen before. He wondered if this was the way they talked sometimes when he and his sister weren't around. His mother turned to Bret. Her face looked normal again.

"Eat that oatmeal before it turns cold," she said. His father got up from the table and left the room. His fork was stuck into the middle of his toast.

Bret couldn't finish the oatmeal. His mother faced the window, looking out onto the front lawn Bret's father had meticulously mowed and edged the day before. "Did Dad kill people in Korea?" Bret asked. He had seen enough war movies to know that ordinary people, people just like his dad, had fought in Europe during World War II and, some years later, in Korea. In the war movies nobody questioned whether the fighting or the killing was right or wrong; it was just something they had to do. Now it was different. Young people, people his sister's age and older, were asking if it was really necessary to fight and to die like that. It made Bret's father angry. His sister had said something about it once. Bret hadn't been paying attention, but suddenly she ran up the stairs in tears and closed herself into the bathroom.

"Don't ever ask him about that," his mother said. "He has enough to think about without bringing that up." She was still gazing out the window.

"But you brought it up," he said.

"My mistake."

He heard his father leave the house through the laundry room. He heard the car start up. Bret and his mother watched his father drive away without kissing them. Bret knew there were things he must never say or his father would get angry. You couldn't talk about Korea and you couldn't talk about the Vietnam protesters. There were other things too, subjects that made Bret's father's cheeks turn red and set him to pacing.

Bret sat down in the grass, in the exact spot he'd been pushed to an hour or so ago. He reviewed it all in his mind. He didn't feel right about it somehow. He was sure now that his father would've wanted him to fight. He hadn't run, not when challenged, yet he hadn't fought. What might have happened if he fought back? He thought if he had fought, and if it looked like Tony were starting to lose, then pirate man and Tony's dad would've done more than just spit, threaten, and push him. To give them what they wanted, to fight, that would surely have made it worse. But to run away. He wouldn't want to go home now if he had run. And, in a sense, that, too, would've been giving them what they wanted. Standing there as he had, that had confused them just as much as he was confused by their behavior.

He had watched a movie with his sister once, about a boy who felt himself being torn apart by his parents and the other kids at school, tough kids who wanted him to be more like them. The boy had said to his father that sometimes you just had to stand up for what you believed, that it was a matter of honor. But his father couldn't help him. He had gotten into trouble, this boy, and had to face it alone. Bret looked over at his sister during this scene and noticed tears in her eyes. Lately, she was always crying. At the time, Bret didn't understand the movie, but he felt it, knew that what the boy in the movie was feeling was real and important. The only other movies that talked about honor were war movies. It was one of those words he wasn't sure he trusted. At the time he was distracted by the red jacket the boy in the movie wore. He wanted one of those.

He stood up and brushed the stray grass and dirt from his jeans. It hadn't hurt at the time, but now his jaw was sore. His face felt tight and a bit swollen under the ears. It hurt when he opened his mouth. He would ask his mother for an aspirin. He would say he had a headache. He was not going to mention Tony or the two grown-ups. It would be too hard to explain anyway. He knew if he told his dad about it, his dad would be disappointed in him — not ashamed of him the way Tony's dad said, but disappointed. And his mother would be so afraid she would not let him out of the house in the afternoon anymore. No. This was the type of thing you kept to yourself.

He walked in the direction of home. He needed to wash up, swallow that aspirin, and work through his math problems in time for dinner. And after dinner he would watch the news special about the election. His father would probably talk back at the television, just as he did during baseball games. Bret would jot his notes and watch carefully. He would try to listen to both Nixon and McGovern. He would find three things to discuss in class tomorrow morning. One of them would be the war in Vietnam. And when he saw his new friends from the football game on the playground at school tomorrow, he would greet them by name. ∎

The Way with Everything

BRET SINGLETON CROSSED the street and ducked down the west aisle of the big commercial tomato patch just opposite his house. He loped along the edge of the irrigation ditch, his Daisy BB rifle in hand, looking down each of the long rows of tomato plants. The farmer and his crew had tied up the bushes to the top rungs of the wooden support trellises last week, so he could now walk upright in the patch without being seen.

The tomatoes were green and growing bigger by the day. Another ten days or so and the field would have spots of orange punctuating the thick green foliage. Only a few days more and the field would be filled with Mexicans in straw hats bobbing up and down the rows as they filled their baskets with the bright red fruit.

Yes, fruit. He had settled an argument with his buddies Cam and Ronny after they insisted that tomatoes were vegetables. He showed them the article in volume seven of *The Book of Knowledge*. The confusion had come from the fact that tomatoes were often cooked and eaten as vegetables, but scientifically they were classified as fruit. "Leave it to Singleton," his friend Ronny had said after seeing the article, "master of totally stupid shit that no one needs to know. What would happen if you applied that mind of yours to something useful, like passing algebra, for instance, or getting to second base with Sheila Kennedy?" He had a point. The things Bret knew were not typically the things that came in handy in the day-to-day lives of most fifth-graders.

Bret listened for the farmer's pick up truck and looked down each of the rows for jackrabbits. It was this time of the afternoon, about an hour before dusk, that they could be spotted leaping from row to row. And it was this time of the afternoon that the farmer most often made his final rounds in his dusty white truck before going home for the night. At about the middle row of the patch, he turned in, avoiding the mud in the low point of the row by angling his tennis shoes against the sides of the mounds. You couldn't move quickly like this, but you could stand upright, not hunched over, as he had to earlier in the summer when the bushes didn't yet reach the top of the trellis.

A big gray jackrabbit appeared out of the corner of his left eye. He cocked his Daisy quickly, brought the barrel up to his eye, and followed the animal as best he could. He squeezed the trigger and felt the rifle pull slightly as he fired. Pop! The rabbit leapt across the row and disappeared into the green. The rabbits were growing, too, as the tomato bushes matured. The farmer, who had a real rifle, a Winchester .22, in the rear window of his pick up, had thinned out their numbers considerably as the summer wore on. There were several days in late June when he'd seen the farmer leap from his truck, rifle in hand, take a knee and fire into the rows. He tossed the corpses into the bed of his truck.

When Bret told his friend Cam about this, Cam wondered aloud what the farmer did with all the corpses.

"Dinner," Bret answered.

"What does rabbit taste like?" Cam asked.

"Like chicken," said Bret, "only tougher."

"You've eaten rabbit?"

"No, but my dad has. In the war. He's also eaten rattlesnake."

"You can eat rattlesnake?"

"Of course. The poison is in the tail, dimwit. You cut off the tail and the head, slice it lengthwise and cook it. But if you cook it too long it tastes like rubber."

"Like a rubber chicken." Cam pretended to hold a cigar next to his mouth in tribute to Groucho Marx. "Eat the rubber chicken and win a hundred dollars."

Bret made a honking noise with his lips and pretended to lift his hat like Groucho's mute brother Harpo.

There were snakes in the tomato patch, but not rattlers. His dad told him you had to go up to the San Gabriel mountains to find those, and even then rattlers were shy creatures. The only time you spotted one was when it eased out onto the road to warm up in the afternoon sun. His dad had been an eagle scout before being drafted into the Korean War. Bret loved to hear his father talk about the strange things he had seen and done before becoming an optometrist.

Bret's dad had bought him the Daisy BB rifle and a 600-pack of BBs for Christmas. He had told Bret never to aim the rifle at a person. This little starter rifle was designed for target-shooting, he had told him, and wasn't good for much more. He could try aiming at birds and other small prey if he wanted, but Bret's dad preferred he not shoot a BB at any living thing. Christmas morning his dad set a row of empty Coors cans up along the back fence for him to practice. It took him awhile to get the hang of it, but after about twenty shots or so he'd been able to plink all the cans off the fence.

Bret continued walking down the row until he reached the middle. By his estimation, he was now in the very heart of the big tomato patch, surrounded by its temporary ecosystem. It was cool and silent here. He sat on the edge of the dirt mound and lay his rifle across his knees. He had begun to think of this as his summer sanctuary. For four months out of the year, from first sprouts in May through final harvest in August, this was his patch; it was directly across from his house, after all, and when Cam and Ronny wanted to play in it, they came to his house and together they crossed the street and entered the patch. And sometimes, like today, when neither Cam nor Ronny was around, he would venture in alone. More and more, he preferred it this way.

Bret listened for the farmer's truck. The drama in which the boys saw themselves as central characters involved the farmer as the villain and they as the heroes — the truck was a tank of Nazi soldiers, and they were Allied infantry troops behind enemy lines. He wanted the drama to be set in the present day, but he knew the North Vietnamese didn't use tanks. From what he'd seen on the evening news, this war was being fought in humid jungles by foot soldiers and by pilots in helicopters and bombers.

Whenever the boys saw or heard the truck, they ran. On foot they could maneuver quickly, zig-zagging in and out of the rows, like soldiers evading a sniper. They spilled into one of the irrigation ditches that surrounded the patch, then ran for the street. Was the farmer actually pursuing them, or was it a coincidence that the truck spat more dust into the air when they were there? By the time the old truck rounded the corner of the patch, the boys were ducking into Bret's garage, where they had hidden a stash of Twinkies and RC Cola.

He lay his head back against the twine that bound the tomato vines to the trellis. A blue jay screeched at him. Two crows cut across the sky. He lifted the Daisy and took aim at them, making an exploding noise with his mouth. Higher overhead he saw a contrail stretching out behind an Air Force jet, a T-38. He'd looked it up one day last spring: a contrail was a trail of vapor emitted from jet engines when flying beyond the 8,000 feet mark, where the air was cold; they consisted of millions of tiny water particles turning into ice crystals. He traced the trail across the sky with his finger, imagining that he had drawn it with the power of his mind.

On the mound next to his sneaker was an ant-hill. Hundreds of nervous red ants swarmed, moving in long lines in and around their nest. Some of them were crawling on his shoe. They seemed especially interested in following the laces up towards his ankle. If Cam or Ronny were here he would demolish the ant-hill beneath his sneaker, destroying the small mound and as many ants as he could crush with the butt of his Daisy. But now he simply sat and watched them. He followed their lines up the tomato vines and across the rough wood of the trellis.

His mother had spent several evenings this summer digging trellis splinters out of his fingers with a pair of tweezers as Bret sat atop the closed toilet lid under the bright bathroom light. "I don't suppose you could wear your dad's gardening gloves when you go into the patch?" she asked. He sat through those sessions with his pocket comb between his teeth, pretending to be a soldier on the operating table while a field surgeon dug bullets from his hide with only a slug of whiskey as anesthetic. After she dug as much of the wood as she could from his flesh, she would coat it with Mercurochrome —the stuff that stung like a wasp and dyed your skin red. Following this last step, Bret's mom blew on the wound to help relieve the sting.

A large black beetle crawled to the top of the mound near him. *Halyomorpha halys,* according to *The Book of Knowledge.* Stink bugs, the boys called them, because when you handled them they lifted their rear and emitted an offensive odor to repel predators. Bret had looked them up, hoping to find some interesting facts to share with Cam and Ronny. But the boys had already discovered all there was to know about them by capturing and torturing them. They collected them in empty RC Cola cans and then dropped matches inside and plugged their noses against the intense odor. The bugs made a sizzling sound as they burned. Stink bug holocaust, they called it.

Bret broke off a piece of wood from the trellis and held it next to the bug. The beetle stopped momentarily, moving its antennae, then crawled out onto the stick. He watched it for awhile, holding the stick up before his eyes to get a close look. "You're an ugly son of a bitch," he said aloud, "but kind of cool in your own way." Bret thought the bug would be a good movie monster, blown up to twenty feet or so, like the giant, atomic ants in *Them!* He imagined this bug reaching the crest of a hill overlooking a sleepy town, the citizens calmly going about their business. Then more giant stink bugs scuttling to the crest of the hill, moving their antennae and making eerie alien noises. They would attack the town, fouling it up with their stink and crushing teenagers in their proboscises. The army would try to blow them up, or burn them with flame-throwers, but the burning bugs would only make the town stink worse. It would take a clever scientist like Edmund Gwenn to figure out the most effective poison. And even though the bugs would be wiped out, the movie would end with a dire warning. How many more humongous bugs were out there, lurking? The stink would never go away, and the poison it took to kill them would taint the water and the crops for years to come.

Bret lowered the stick and watched the bug crawl back onto the soil. He had an urge to bring the stick down onto the bug like a knife, impaling it like the insects pinned to the display case in his classroom at school. Would it make a noise as he killed it? Would it ooze green slime? Before he could decide, he saw movement in the soil the next row over. It was a garter snake, with a sort of checkered brown pattern and long yellow stripes running down each side. It had a bulge in the middle of its long body; probably it was digesting one of the many rats Bret had seen emerging from the drainage ditch just before dark. The snake was stretched out along the base of the row, next to the mud, moving at a good clip. Probably it had not even seen Bret. He watched it as it undulated down the row and eventually went out of sight. He would look up garter snakes tonight in *The Book of Knowledge*.

There was no end of things to be learned. You could spend your life just learning stuff, watching, observing. Then what? What would you do with all the things you had learned, Bret wondered. He thought of the monks that Mr. Stevens, his teacher, had told them about, who lived in large stone monasteries during the Middle Ages, keeping knowledge alive when the world around them lived in ignorance, disease, and darkness. It was still out there — ignorance, disease, darkness. Granted, he hadn't seen much of it first-hand, but he'd heard about it. The war was going on in the jungles of Vietnam, a far away place of rice farmers and Buddhist monks and Communists. There were race riots just a little way up the freeway in Watts. There were huge protests of scary-looking hippies in Washington, D. C. President Nixon had declared war on cancer, a disease he had looked up recently because Mr. Stevens had developed it in his lungs and had taken a leave of absence in the middle of the school year to go to the Mayo Clinic. The world didn't seem any less dangerous just because the bubonic plague wasn't around anymore.

Standing out on the blacktop one day, Mr. Stevens had asked a group of boys what they would want to be had they lived during the Middle Ages — farmer, knight, landlord, monk. There weren't many choices. But the boys had answered knights because at least then you could have weapons and ride horses instead of hoeing in the muddy fields all day long like the farmers or hanging around a cold castle like the lords and ladies. Not long afterward, Bret, Cam, and Ronny had formed a short-lived club called the Knights of Fountain Valley. But secretly Bret preferred the monks. As a knight, you could too easily end up on the working end of a lance.

Granted, the life of the monk seemed dull by comparison, and those brown frocks looked itchy in the extreme, but Bret thought he preferred security and longevity to adventure.

He heard the farmer's truck engine coming down the west aisle. He quickly curled himself beneath the tomato bushes, tucking his legs in over his head, like a stink bug on its back, a move he had learned from the soldiers on *Combat*, his dad's favorite TV show. The Sarge and his squad often hid from Kraut convoys in roadside shrubs or hung in the rafters of countryside barns in total silence while the enemy searched for them.

He lay his gun at the base of the trench and waited for the truck to pass. The truck sat idling at the end of the row. Bret peeked his head over just enough to see that the truck was stopped. But the squeaky door had not sprung open. Maybe the farmer was lighting a cigarette. Bret tried to control his breathing and wondered what he would do if the farmer spotted him. Would it be better to hunker down and hope that he would drive on, or leap out and make a run for it? The more he tried to quiet himself, the more fidgety he became. He was getting a cramp in his right leg. His breath was coming faster and shallower and, no doubt, louder.

He heard the truck kick into gear and continue on up the aisle. Bret rolled out from under cover and straightened his leg, dragging it through the mud in the process and messing up his jeans. He would hear the old complaint again tonight from his mother as he slipped off his dirt-caked jeans and draped them over the hamper: "Why does playing in the tomato patch have to involve you rolling around in the dirt? I've seen that farmer's jeans. They're cleaner than yours and he spends his whole day in there."

Out of the corner of his eye, another jackrabbit leapt. When he turned toward it, he saw there were two young rabbits. They had stopped very nearby when Bret had been frozen beneath the tomato bushes. They were nibbling some of the green tomatoes that, he now noticed, were just beginning to turn color. It was the first spot of red he had seen this season.

Bret pulled his gun into his lap. The rabbits looked up nervously, but they had apparently not spotted him. He sat as still as he could, realizing that he had to pee. The ants were crawling on his socks now, and one or two of them began to bite at his ankle. Between his bladder and the ants, he realized that he would not be able to hold still for long. Worse, he had forgotten to cock his rifle after the last discharge. The metallic clack of the lever would surely scare them away. At that moment a squawking murder of crows passed directly overhead. He quickly cocked the rifle and lifted it to his right eye, closing his left. He silently thanked the crows for covering his noisy preparations with their loud caws. Both rabbits were still feeding. He lined up the nearest rabbit down the barrel. He aimed at the base of the rabbit's ear and pulled the trigger. With the loud pop, the other rabbit took off in a flash, leaping, in its confusion, right past him, close enough for Bret to reach out and touch had his reflexes been quick enough.

But he held tight to the gun. The young rabbit lay twitching in the dirt. Bret had never actually hit anything before. In fact, he had begun to assume that the BBs were harmless because all he had ever managed to do was scare off rabbits and birds with the noise of the rifle. He knew the BB would sting, but he didn't expect one to actually take down an animal. He stood over the rabbit, who lay on its side with its rear legs moving as if it were bounding through the patch. There was a bubble of red goo at its neck, right near the spot where he had aimed.

The animal was suffering. His first thought was the racehorse movies he had watched on television. The trainers in those movies always recommended "putting the animal out of its misery" when wounded. It was the humane thing to do. He took aim at the center of the animal and squeezed the trigger. The trigger pulled too easily and Bret realized he had not cocked the gun. He fumbled with the lever, pulling it clumsily away from the stock and pushing it back against it. Again he aimed and fired the gun. Immediately following the pop, the rabbit began to cry out. He had put a BB into its ribs at very close range. The rabbit sounded like a human infant, its cry coming in loud, wheezy screeches. Bret froze. The sound terrified him. Without thinking, he cocked the rifle again and put another BB into the animal's hide. The cry intensified. Instead of putting the animal out of its misery, he was inflicting more pain. His stomach felt like it had flipped inside-out.

He turned and walked away as swiftly as he could given the narrowness and depth of the irrigation row. He aimed his body for the daylight at the end of the row. One of his sneakers popped off at the heel. He kept walking, trying to run, stumbling against the sides of the wooden trellis. He could hear the wood snapping as he pushed against the trellis in an effort to keep himself upright. A sharp, acidic taste came into Bret's mouth.

He was going to vomit. He wanted to get to the end of the row and to vomit into the irrigation ditch. Maybe the rabbit would be dead by then. But the screech of the rabbit continued.

He didn't realize until he reached the end of the row that the farmer was standing there. Startled, Bret stopped in his tracks right in front of the farmer. Somehow he had thought the man was bigger and brawnier. But up close Bret saw that he had a slight build, with skinny dark arms protruding from the rolled up sleeves of his denim shirt. His straw hat was frayed and tattered. The eyes that met Bret's eyes were gray and tired but not angry, not malicious. As he stood in front of the farmer, Bret felt dizzy.

The farmer took Bret by his arm and guided him across the irrigation ditch. Bret's eyes were stinging and he couldn't seem to catch his breath. The farmer leaned Bret against his truck, grabbed something from its front seat, and disappeared into the patch. Through his tears, Bret could see the man hobbling down the row toward the noise, which had not let up in the time it had taken Bret to reach the end of the row. In fact, the sound seemed to rise up from the patch in a weird cackle that reminded Brett of a horror movie sound effect. Bret sat down in the dirt and leaned his head back against the rear tire of the truck. He heard the single report of the farmer's rifle, and the rabbit fell silent. Then he heard a second rifle report.

When the farmer emerged from the row a few moments later, two rabbits dangled limply from his left hand. He held them by their back feet. He tossed their corpses over Bret's head and into the bed of his truck, where they landed among a stack of burlap. The farmer opened the door of his cab and put his rifle away, emerging with a Tupperware jug of water. He sat in the dirt next to Bret and took a long swig from the jug. Then he passed it to Bret. "Swish some of this around in your mouth," he told Bret.

Bret never shared drinks, not even with Cam or Ronny; he knew how many germs inhabited the average person's saliva. Nevertheless, he lifted the jug to his lips and sloshed some water into his mouth. He swished it the way his father did with mouthwash, and then he spat the water out between his feet. He slipped his thumb into the heel of his sneaker and pulled it back into place.

Bret passed the jug back to the farmer, who splashed some water out into his palm. He gently put his wet hand to Bret's forehead. Then he repeated the action on the back of Bret's neck. It was the same thing his mother did with a wet washrag when he had the flu. His breathing came easier now.

The farmer picked up Bret's Daisy from the dirt. He pulled a blue bandanna from around his neck and wiped the stock and the barrel clean. "Never did like these BB guns," the farmer said. "A gun should never be viewed as a toy." He handed Bret his clean rifle. "That's my philosophy, for what it's worth," he said.

"My dad gave it to me," Bret said. "He told me not to shoot at living creatures."

"I guess you can see now why he told you that."

"I feel a little sick," Bret said.

"You'll feel better soon. Just sit a spell."

"I'm sorry." Bret looked over at the farmer, whose skin was sun-baked and heavily wrinkled. From a distance he appeared to be the same age as Bret's father, but up close he looked nearer in age to his grandfather.

"What are you sorry for?" asked the farmer.

"I'm not sure. For playing in your tomato patch. For hurting that rabbit. I don't know. I just feel guilty and stupid."

The farmer took off his straw hat and wiped the sweat from his brow with his bandanna. Then he soaked the bandanna with water from his jug and squeezed out the excess. He wrapped the wet bandanna around Bret's neck. "That'll cool you off."

Bret nodded. He was finished crying now, and his breath was coming smoother.

The farmer asked, "How old are you, son?"

"Eleven."

"Tall for eleven. I've got a boy almost twice your age."

"Is he in college?" Bret asked.

"He and school don't exactly get along. He's in Vietnam now."

Bret considered this. The picture that appeared in his mind was from a television program he had seen about a platoon of American soldiers fighting their way through the dense jungles. One of their regular tasks was to crawl into the tunnels they found in the forest floor and root out the enemy. "Are you worried about him?"

"He's pretty good at taking care of himself. But, yes, I worry. He's a good shot."

"Did you teach him how to shoot?"

The farmer nodded. "Right here in this tomato patch. With that rifle there that I carry in my truck and still use. One day about five summers ago he bagged an even dozen."

"What did you do with them all?"

"Gave them away to neighbors mostly. We get pretty sick of eating rabbit in our house." The farmer took another gulp of water from his jug. "That rabbit's scream is a defense mechanism. In the wild, that sound would have the same effect on a predator as it did on you, unless it was a cougar. Noises don't stop a cougar, but sometimes they delay it just long enough for the rabbit to get away."

"Did I see you had two of them?"

"Sometimes when they cry out like that the mate stays nearby."

Bret felt a surge of anger at himself. Disgusted, he kicked his rifle into the irrigation ditch. Immediately he saw what an empty and childish gesture this was. He wanted to run, but he knew that would be even more childish. Instead, he blurted out a question he'd wanted to ask his father: "What do you know about cancer?"

"Enough that the word itself gives me the willies. Do you know someone with cancer?"

"My teacher from last year. He left at Christmastime. His wife came to visit our class in the spring. We wrote him a get well soon card and she came to thank us. She kept saying how our note raised his spirits. When we asked her when he was coming back to school she stopped talking. I mean, she couldn't speak anymore. It was like her throat closed up or something. You could tell she had more to say, but . . . ."

The farmer used the toe of his left boot to flick some mud from the heel of his right. "It's a messed up world, isn't it?"

Bret nodded. "Am I in trouble?"

"That depends. How do you feel about tomatoes?"

"I like them in spaghetti sauce."

"Well, so long as you never steal more from this patch than you can cook into a spaghetti sauce, you're not in trouble."

The farmer stood and brushed the dust from his jeans. "I'm about done for today. Do you live nearby?"

"Right across the street."

"Your dad will notice if you don't bring that BB gun home."

"I could tell him I lost it."

"Is that what you'd want your son to tell you if you were a father?"

"I never thought about it that way."

"If you lose the rifle, that'll hurt your father. If you keep it, you're afraid it'll remind you of the suffering of that rabbit. And for a while, it would. So which is the better choice?" The farmer didn't pause to wait for Bret's answer. "If you'd shot it cleanly with a real gun, the rabbit wouldn't have suffered. See, that's what I mean by viewing the gun as a toy. If you'd been carrying a real rifle, you might feel sorry for killing that animal, as you should. But you would not have been the cause of its suffering."

Bret picked up the rifle. "I'm going to remember the rabbit's cry whether or not I keep this." Overhead a jet engine roared, its contrail crossing the previous fading trail. The sky was darkening. "I hope your son will come home safe," Bret said.

"I hope the same for your teacher."

As the farmer climbed into his truck, Bret began to walk down the aisle next to the drainage ditch.

The farmer leaned his head out the window. "How would you like a job picking these tomatoes when they come ripe?"

Bret looked back. "I'll have to ask my dad."

"Let me know what he says."

Bret nodded. He heard the truck start up. The tires spat a dust cloud behind him as the farmer drove away. Bret walked down the east aisle of the patch towards home. The crows cawed at him from the line of eucalyptus along the edge of the patch. Crows were smarter than other birds, he remembered. According to *The Book of Knowledge*, they lived in the same place their whole lives and made a wide variety of verbalizations. They were annoying nevertheless. He wondered briefly if the crows were trying to communicate with him. If he were a crow, what would he want to say to the humans in his neighborhood?

He realized that he still wore the farmer's bandanna. Well, he would throw it into the hamper with his dirty jeans. It was Friday, so his favorite television shows were on tonight, even though they were summer repeats. His mom had promised to cook spaghetti and meatballs. He would help her by spreading the butter and garlic on the bread and tossing the salad.

He came to the street. Before crossing, he turned and looked back at the tomato patch. The setting sun made the clouds look orange and pink, a phenomenon caused by dust particles and aerosols in the atmosphere. Bret had written a paper on the subject for Mr. Steven's class, which he entitled, "The Startling Beauty of Clouds Under the Influence of Airborne Pollutants." Next to the A- at the top of the page, Mr. Stevens had written: "Your affinity for such beauty is what makes you Bret Singleton and no one else." Mr. Stevens was always making comments like that. Who used the word "affinity" anyway? The long-term substitute who replaced him, Mrs. Williams, wrote only "good job" on his papers, next to a hastily sketched smiley face.

It was a messed up world, but there were the orange and pink clouds at sunset. If he were a monk he would be returning to his cell for evening prayers now. Maybe he would write a poem in Latin about the color of the sky. Or maybe he would sketch some clouds in the margins of a sacred text he was copying. Centuries later some scholar would take note of the monk with an affinity for such beauty.

He crossed the street and entered his garage, leaning the rifle in the corner next to his bike. Cam and Ronny had said something about going to the beach Saturday. The beach would be a good change of pace. Even if crows were smarter, he preferred sea gulls. The sea gulls could fly for miles out to sea without growing tired. They had been known to land on the backs of humpbacks and pluck out pieces of whale flesh to sustain themselves.

He pulled a can of RC cola from his stash and took a long drink, enjoying the sweetness of the cola on his tongue and the intensity of the carbonation as it burned his throat. He was beginning to see that this was the way with everything: color and pollution, gulls and crows, sweetness and burning. Things were mixed together, the good with the bad, and you had to learn to take them that way — to see the good in the bad, if possible, and maybe even the bad in the good.

As he finished off the cola and tossed the empty into the trash bin, he noticed his pants were wet. Well, that hadn't happened in a while. Not since first grade or so. He must have peed himself in the midst of the rabbit debacle. He would have to hurry past his mom and hide the jeans somewhere until they dried. He wondered how much the farmer would pay him to pick tomatoes. He imagined himself bobbing among the other straw hats in the field, filling the baskets and carrying them to the end of the row, emptying the baskets into the bed of the big truck that hauled the tomatoes north for sale.

He was pretty sure he would hear the rabbit's cry again tonight. It would be tough to get to sleep at the usual time, even with the distraction of his TV shows. He would take a volume of *The Book of Knowledge* and a flashlight to bed with him again. He had some questions about garter snakes. He thought he should look up the entry on Vietnam, too. A day at the beach would be a good thing to look forward to. ∎

Gravidation

LATELY MY BLADDER has become my master. I must serve it before I can do anything else. I've even begun to pee my panties just a bit when I laugh or cough. It's not to the public embarrassment stage yet. From what my sister Peg tells me — she's six years my senior — that's coming.

When I spoke to her on the phone Sunday afternoon she told me her doctor has recommended surgery. Next week she will have a bladder sling inserted. The doctor told her that by lifting the bladder and urethra, the sling will relieve the leaks and ease the urgency to go. We laughed together about how gravity is the enemy of women on the outside and on the inside. But our laughter was more of a nervous release than anything else. There is nothing particularly funny about surgery. Still, it felt good to laugh with my Peg. Peg o' My Heart, I call her, after the famous old song. Our father owned the Dean Martin recording, and he used to invite Peg to dance to it whenever the needle came around to that song. That's one of my earliest memories, Peg and our father dancing in the living room with Dean Martin crooning on the hi-fi. Even over the telephone, our nervous laughter caused her to squirt some pee into her panties, and that caused her to swear and laugh even more. I had to put my hand over my mouth to stifle my laughter so she could calm down and stop leaking into her panties.

So first I pee, then I come out to the kitchen and pour myself a glass of Pinot Grigio, stand here at the window, sipping. There's my husband Jerry out there on the back patio, doing his daily meditation. He's seated on his little pillow, his back to me, facing the lawn. God, he has such lovely broad shoulders. You can really appreciate a man's shoulders when he controls his waistline. So many men, when they reach middle- age, get that paunch that draws your attention away from other features. Here's his journal here, on the kitchen counter. He leaves it out for me to read while I'm preparing our dinner. I often prop it open like a cookbook.

My husband has taken a vow of silence. Well, not a vow exactly. He fell silent when he lost his job at the YMCA. It was the third job in three years he'd lost, each one a rung lower in pay, status, and satisfaction. For a dozen years Jerry worked as a copywriter for Howard & Howard, an advertising agency with several big retail clothing accounts. But when the firm shifted its leadership from father to son, my Jerry found himself shifted out of a job for the first time since college. Then he worked for two years managing a small fleet of limousines. But that company went bust when the economy tanked and gas prices went through the roof. Also, it was revealed that at least two of the drivers were mobile pimps, using the limos as portable motel rooms for their "ladies."

After six months of searching, Jerry took a job in charge of fundraising and membership recruitment at the Y, a job for which he had no talent and no passion. He came home the day the Y released him and sank into the recliner in our living room. As I approached him, he waved his hands in front of himself as if waving off an airplane from a bad landing. He traced the sign of the cross with his thumb on his lips. That was nine months ago.

Since then, he fills his days with the same five activities:

1. He listens to music in a minor key. He likes his Mahler in the morning and his Erik Satie in the afternoon. He'll put on *Gymnopedies*, for example, sit in the recliner and close his eyes, touching his fingertips one-by-one to his thumbs in rhythm with the music.

2. He practices zazen on the back patio. He tosses a small pillow on the pavement, lights some incense, and sits facing south, away from the house. He finds a focal point in the grass, and breathes as evenly as a body can — in and out, in and out.

3. He takes long walks in the hills above our home. I have accompanied him on occasion. He hikes at a good pace for a middle-aged guy, marches right up the hill to the promontory, sits on the bench overlooking the valley, and watches the hawks as they surf the thermals.

4. He fills one page — and one page only — in his journal each day. When I arrive home from my shift at the retirement home, the first thing I do is read that day's journal page. Actually, it's the second or the third thing. Peeing comes first. I pee out the poison of my workday. Then I pour

my glorious glass of Pinot Grigio. Then I read his page. It's our way of staying in touch, since only one of us speaks. It's probably enough, though. If you think about it . . . if each of us reserved our daily communication to one carefully written page per day, just think how much worthless chatter would be eliminated from our lives.

5. He watches his daily episode of *The Joy of Painting*, a show that has been re- running on PBS for umpteen years. The fuzzy and soft-spoken artist paints a brand new picture every episode, in just thirty minutes. Peg o' My Heart says she tried to watch this show but found it cloying and monotonous. The painter says the same things episode after episode, and all he paints are landscapes. But Jerry watches this painter the way some people watch the Pope or the Dalai Lama.

Near as I can tell, unless he's got a secret stash of calories somewhere, Jerry eats about the same amount of food as the robins and jays that flit upon the lawn as he sits cross-legged on his little pillow in the backyard. I, however, have taken food as my lover, since Jerry is not only silent but celibate, too. Every evening, while Jerry breathes and breathes, staring at his patch of our back lawn while his thoughts drift by like a lazy stream, I cook and drink, cook and drink. And so, in the past nine months, I have grown fat while he, my own little Jack Sprat, has grown thin.

In fact, about six months into this, a rumor started at work that I was pregnant. One day a new resident beamed at my belly and innocently asked, "When are you due?"

"I'm not pregnant," I answered, "just fat."

Peg thinks I should complain to Jerry about my lot. I suppose most wives would complain bitterly if they faced what I face at work and then came home to the perpetual silent treatment. And under more ordinary circumstances I might be one of those wives. But Jerry's silence isn't aimed at me; he speaks to no one. And his silence, it turns out, is a kind of antidote to a toxin that has come into my work life.

The name of this particular toxin is Anna Gustafson, a resident whose creeping dementia is causing her great bitterness. She can't shut up. She blathers on and on. As we say in the nurse's break room, she's lost her edit button. Whatever vile thought enters her mind comes bubbling out like a sulfurous verbal geyser. The best we can do is keep our more vulnerable residents out of her path.

Springer Retirement Community is a two-tiered facility. Most residents reside in the independent living wing, in which they occupy their own little apartments, gather in the commons for activities, and eat together in the dining hall. The second tier is a nursing facility, in which the residents are really patients, who live in double-occupancy rooms watched over by a round-the-clock nursing staff. That's where I work. The other nurses in our facility have given me charge of Anna Gustafson because I have the most experience with dementia patients. If a patient gets a full-blown Alzheimer's diagnosis, they move on to another facility, but in that gray area after they are able to live independently but before they become a possible danger to themselves or others, they stay with us. In the break room, we affectionately refer to our wing as the loony bin.

My own mother drifted in and out of lucidity in her last two years. One day she'd be fine, and the next she'd pop back and forth in time. Time is a slippery thing to the aged. One moment she'd be a little girl on a farm in west Texas, the next moment a bored housewife obsessed with 1970's soap operas, and the next a young woman awaiting the return of her new husband from the war in the Pacific. My ability to manage these shifts and soothe patients as they fight against their own confusion is what gained me the dubious honor of "expert."

This morning, as I went in to strip the sheets from her bed, the lovely Mrs. Gustafson let out with a stream of profanity that would shame any sailor. "Get your flabby ass out of here," she yelled, "you blankety-blank slant-eyed blankety-blank. Quick now, before I call the Sheriff and have him blank you with his blankety-blank billy club. Go back to China, why don't you, you blankety-blank daughter of a chain-gang whore!"

I think maybe what triggered this particular fit was that she had soiled her sheets again. Deep down, she was embarrassed over the mess she had made and angry at her body's regular betrayals. What I do when she flips on that particular switch — the one with the random racial slurs and the sexual insults — is I switch my mind off. I hear her (they can hear her in San

Diego) but I don't register what she's saying. I've trained my mind to just let the sounds roll by, like a muddy stream. Maybe I picked this up from Jerry's zazen practice. I don't fish for anything in that ugly, murky stream; I just watch it bubble and gurgle on by.

In this case I hummed a little tune to myself while she ranted. I hummed the little complex melody of Satie's *Gymnopedies* while I gathered the stinky sheets and put them into the hamper, opened her window, and sprayed the room with Fabrese.

Peg o' My Heart wonders aloud if I am a healer or an enabler. My supervisor at Springer, Franny, says this is an issue every caretaker must address. Every healer, says Franny, is wounded herself, and needs healing herself. We are all walking wounded. We all participate in the world's great sadness. No one is immune, though some are in denial. So says Franny. So say I. Peg thinks I should get right up into Anna Gustafson's face and yell right back. She thinks I might just shout her into polite silence. As my Jerry used to say before his vow of silence, "That's not how I roll."

So my days are spent knee-deep in physical and verbal shit. Despite my attempts to deflect them, some days the things Anna Gustafson says have a way of bypassing my coping strategy. Some days her poison enters my bloodstream, sickening me in body and in spirit. On those days I awaken in the middle of the night with her vile comments ringing in my ears. When that happens, I get up and pour myself a glass of wine and flip through the back pages of Jerry's daily journal. I read his journal the way some people read poetry. Or I open my bible, trolling for wisdom. Lately I've been reading the third chapter of *Ecclesiastes*, which is a poem that encourages us to see the big picture; it says there is a time for everything under heaven, and then the poet catalogs a series of opposites — there is a time to kill, he says, and a time to heal, a time to weep and a time to laugh, and so on. One of the verses says there is a time to keep silence and a time to speak. The back and forth movement of the poem, like a metronome, soothes me, dulls the pain — well, that and the wine, and Jerry's marvelous journal scribblings, which, frankly, are just as nurturing, in their own way, as *Ecclesiastes*.

Up late one night last week I turned on the television to a PBS production of *Hamlet*. I've never read the play, so I'm afraid much of it was lost on me. It was pleasant enough to look at, with richly-textured period costumes and beautiful actors. And the language—who knows what most of it means?—just poured over me, like I was standing under a shower of words. At one point Hamlet turned to the camera and proclaimed, "Lately, I have lost all my mirth." And this was exactly what Jerry had written that day in his journal. My dear, sweet, unemployed husband has lost his joy. Everyone who knows him knows this. Unlike Hamlet, however, he is not considering suicide. There is no *to be or not to be* in his pages. If it weren't for his journal, I wouldn't know this. In fact, I've learned more about my husband in these months of silence than I ever knew—or would ever have known.

In his journal, he records his encounters with nature in heartbreaking detail. On his walks in the hills, he observes birds, animals, plants, trees, clouds. My Jerry knows the names of all these things. He imagines that he communes with them. Who was it?— St. Francis, I believe, who preached to the birds. My Jerry has no gospel to preach, but he and those animals are communicating on a deep level. His journal has become to him his priest, psychologist, friend, confidant. Also, maybe, wife. Part of me longs to hear his spoken voice; however, I'm a little afraid that if he begins to speak again, he will cease to write. Selfishly, I wish to hear him. But if I could be more unselfish—more like St. Francis—I would wish for him continued silence.

I stand at the kitchen window, unloading groceries, staring at his broad back as he sits on his cushion, gazing vaguely at his patch of lawn. He sneezes, wipes his nose on his sleeve. He rings the little bell next to his cushion, crosses himself, bows to the setting sun. The smoke from his incense trails into the air and is caught by the breeze. The interesting thing about Jerry is he went from having no religion to embracing all of them at once. He goes to mass at the little church around the corner, he does his Zen thing, and he's reading up on Native American shamanism, as well as the Hindu *Vedas*. It's like he's catching up for all his years of getting and spending. I wonder now if he'll ever go back to work. One thing we've discovered over the past nine months is that we can live on my salary alone. It's not easy, but it's possible.

My sister Peg asks me if I resent Jerry, now that I am the breadwinner.

I answer her that not only am I the breadwinner, I'm also the bread baker and the bread eater, since Jerry consumes so little. I don't believe he has used his ATM card in the past nine months. He will need a new pair of hiking boots soon, since he's nearly worn out his current pair. In his journal he has written that Henry David Thoreau pared down life to its essentials: food, clothing, shelter. I've never read *Walden*, but I'll bet Jerry matches him for austerity of lifestyle. And my Jerry's a writer, too, even if I am his only reader. Do I resent him? No. He may be depressed and listless, but he's got this personal discipline going that I really respect. And then there are those broad shoulders.

Peg o' My Heart would never understand me if I told her how much inspiration I draw from him. She once whispered the word *deadbeat* during one of our weekly phone conversations. I pretended like I didn't hear it. After a pause, we went on to talk about the strange weather that's been hitting the Midwest this year — the way the quick snow melt has raised so many rivers to flood stage. On days like today I'd like to retreat into Jerry's daily routine, or discover my own. My routine would have to include cooking, cleaning, and paying the bills. I might replace Mahler with Schubert. I might take up yoga. My supervisor, Franny, swears by it. She goes to the yoga center two nights a week and on Saturday mornings. She talks a lot about centering, Franny does, how yoga centers her. I'm due for some centering, that's for sure.

After cleaning and chopping the veggies, I carry our wine glasses into the back bedroom. Jerry has switched on his television guru; the fuzzy and soft-spoken artist has wet his canvas with Liquid White and loaded his palette with color. Jerry lays propped on two pillows. The artist dabs his two-inch brush into the Titanium White, mixes in some Phthalo Blue with a swipe of Liquid Black, moving the brush in a swirling motion, out of a vanishing point about three-quarters up the canvas.

I hand Jerry his wine and join him on the bed. I set my glass over on the end table and cuddle up to him for the first time in a long while. Normally, I hand him his wine and go cook. But tonight I lie down. He makes room for me, adjusting his legs to allow me to scoot up next to him. I settle my head on his chest just beneath his left arm. He's got some body odor going, my Jerry, because he showers less these days. But it's not an offensive odor — certainly no worse than what I encounter at work everyday — he's just a bit ripe with dried sweat and incense.

The artist dips his brush into some Cadmium Yellow and enlarges the swirls. Then he daubs into a little Yellow Ocher. I can see now what he's doing. It is a sun in a misty mountain sky. Who knew the sky contained so many colors? Come to think of it, when was the last time I looked at the sky? — I mean really looked, not just glanced in order to divine the weather.

The artist speaks in hushed tones, as if he were revealing the secrets of creation, as if he spoke too loud the little magic spell of his painting would be broken, the harsh TV studio lights would brighten to the point of white-out and he would disappear. Jerry lay next to me perfectly relaxed, his breathing deep and even. He takes a sip of wine. If Jerry were a cat, he'd be purring right now.

The fuzzy, soft-spoken painter takes up another brush and outlines a mountain range just beneath his sun. He dips his knife into the Van Dyke Brown and the Midnight Black, creating a dark bead along the tip of the knife. He scrapes the paint across the canvas to get the texture right. "Remember where your light source is," he says. "Always know where the light is coming from. That way you know where your shadows live."

He takes up the first brush again and dips it into a pail of thinner, then he shakes it, smacking the brush from side to side against the leg of his easel. He smiles broadly. "Just beat the devil out of that brush," he says, unable to suppress the mischievous grin that shines through his whiskers. Such joy this little game brings him! I can't help but smile along with him. Jerry's tummy shakes a little; I realize he is laughing. It's a muffled little laugh, but it rises from clear down in the belly.

The artist loads his clean brush with Indian Yellow and Bright Red, daubing in highlights around the sunny side of his mountains. He asks, "See how that adds depth? That's what we're after. We want to push those mountains back a bit and make room for what's coming next."

He switches to a #6 fan brush, drags it through the Dark Sienna. Suddenly there are dark evergreens on those mountains. Jerry groans with satisfaction. The world of the picture is emerging from just a few deft strokes, with just a few colors from the edges of his palate: the hazy sun in the distance beyond the mountains, the forest coming down the mountainsides, the mist in the trees.

I feel my body relax and mold itself around Jerry's body; like fetal twins, my legs melt into his legs, my belly rests against his hips, my breasts touch the side of his stomach, where his love handles used to be. I swear our breathing has slipped into perfect sync. The artist slides a dry two-inch brush lightly across the middle of the canvas. "Just two hairs and some air is all you need. There," he whispers, "the sunlight filters through the trees."

The artist straightens his back and looks at his painting. "All right," he says, "now let's have some fun. Let's put a little cabin in here." He cleans his brush again by dipping it into the thinner, shaking the brush, then slapping it again against the leg of his easel. It sounds like the tail of a beaver thumping against a log. He drags his clean brush through the Sap Green, Van Dyke Brown, and Indian Yellow. "You're going to think I'm crazy," he says, "but look how this cabin just appears when I go like this." He creates a roof line with the tip of the brush, then pulls the brush down in neat, vertical strokes. I swear it looks like wooden planks catching the distant sunlight. Then he loads the edge of his knife with Midnight Black and Phthalo Blue, the same colors that originally brought the sky to life, and creates wood grain. "See how that adds just the right texture?"

You can't help but share in the joy of his creation. Twenty minutes earlier, the fuzzy, soft-spoken man stood before a blank canvas. And now there is a dilapidated cabin in a grassy clearing. With quick, careless strokes he highlights shrubbery in the foreground with the tip of his one-inch brush. He paints a little stream that drops right off the lower edge of the canvas. Your eye goes up and back from the little cabin, to the forested mountains, to the hazy sun just atop their dark peaks. He has made a world that I feel I can walk into. I close my eyes and hear the trickle of the stream, the buzz of insects, the twittering of birds, and the warmth of that sun peeking over the shoulders of those distant mountains. The world of the painting slowly takes over the world of the pudgy, burned-out caregiver and her depressed, unemployed husband lying on a sagging mattress in the twilight of an autumn evening. When I look again, the fuzzy, soft-spoken artist is dragging his largest brush right down through much of the detail he has so artfully created. But when he switches to the fan brush and begins to leaf in branches and then the highlights, I see the wisdom in such a bold move.

I thought it was wonderful before. Now I see occur what he'd been talking about all along — with this new addition, a kind of radical depth emerges. "Never paint a lone tree," he says, putting in another big trunk. "Trees are just like people; they need friends. Always give your tree a friend. Go ahead and mingle their branches," he says. "Ever notice how trees will grow into each other?" Then he picks up a tiny brush and slips it into Bright Red. "Let's call this one finished," he says, signing his name atop a cluster of shadowy shrubs in the corner.

When I awaken it is dark and I am alone on the bed. The news is on the TV, sound muted. The smiling news anchors are reporting another shooting up in Oakland. Another child has been caught in gangster crossfire. The sliding glass door stands wide open. The crickets serenade me. The smiling weather girl takes over, pointing at places on her map where raindrops have been spotted. A nice breeze cools the bedroom. The wind chimes on our back porch are playing a spirited little tune. I have been dreaming in vivid color, which is rare for me. Whenever I remember my dreams (and I haven't recalled any lately) they are usually in black & white.

In my dream, I was standing at the kitchen sink, as usual. Jerry was seated on his pillow, as usual; however, in my dream he was facing me instead of having his back to me. Suddenly he began to levitate. He lifted slowly into the air to a height of about eight feet and hovered there. Beneath him stood Anna Gustafson and Peg o' My Heart. Anna was hopping on both feet, straining to reach Jerry's pillow. Peg had a bucket of rocks that she was chucking at him. They both wanted to knock him out of the sky. Jerry seemed impervious. I tried to shout a warning to him but couldn't make a sound. When I looked at the food I had been chopping on the kitchen counter, there among the veggies and the raw meat lay my tongue. As disturbing as this sounds, when I awaken I am not agitated or afraid.

Instead, I feel rested, even though I've only been asleep for about an hour.

I have to pee. But I force myself to lie still, holding it in. If I practice this the way Jerry practices zazen, maybe I can hold off the inevitable bladder sling in my future with sheer discipline. The covers next to me are still warm where Jerry had lain. The smiling sports guy on the TV news shakes his head and scolds the Giants' pitcher for walking too many batters. They have edited together a little comic silent movie of Arizona Diamondbacks walking and walking from base to base while the pitcher wipes and wipes the sweat from his brow. Where has Jerry gone? It is not his usual pattern at all to arise after his art episode. In my Jerry's daily routine, the fuzzy, soft-spoken artist is always followed by a nap, while I watch the night come on from the warmly-lit kitchen.

I give in to my bladder. Then I scuff down the dark hallway towards the light. I stand in the archway to the kitchen, squinting. My Jerry is preparing dinner. He opens the rice cooker; a wave of fragrant steam rises. The timer beeps. He grabs a hot pad and peeks in the oven. I can't remember the last time he cooked for me. Aside from the five elements of his daily routine, he hasn't done much of anything lately. I'm still thinking about my dream, and for a moment I wonder if it's possible I'm still asleep. But who pees in a dream?

When Jerry sees me leaning against the fridge, yawning and scratching like a man, he pours me a fresh glass of Pinot Grigio. He is humming the happy melody of Beethoven's Sixth. I clumsily get down some plates from the cupboard while he pulls the roaster from the oven. He uses the big, two-pronged fork to hold the chicken in place while he carves it with our only sharp knife. He divides up the pieces between our plates. Taking the slotted spoon, he scoops out some veggies from the roasting pan — carrots, potatoes, onions, celery, apples. Apples? Where did Jerry get such an idea?

I sit at the breakfast counter. A huge moth comes to rest on the window screen, stretching her wings, bathing in light. I look around for Jerry's daily journal; it was right here when I came home. Finally I spot it beneath the roasting pan, covered in chicken broth, ruined. Jerry puts a full plate before each of us. He pours some wine into his own glass and lifts it with a flourish. "Let's call this one finished," he says. And for a moment I feel I may levitate. I may lift right off the stool I'm sitting on and float recklessly around the room. ∎

The Haiku Master's Wife

JUST BEFORE DAWN I hear the side gate open and close, and then a rustle
on the back porch as he drops his knapsack, leans his staff against the fence,
and spits into the koi pond. I hear his hiking boots drop, one at a time, into
the gravel. He clucks his tongue at the next-door neighbor's chickens, who
began to scurry when he came into the yard. If I were standing at the kitchen
window, I would see him squat for the key beneath the back door mat and put
it precisely — on the first attempt — into the keyhole. The man has the night
vision of a jaguar. Unfortunately, when he comes home like this from a long
journey, he smells like a baboon, and so rather than stink up the sheets of our
bed, as a kindness to me, he sleeps on the slate floor until I get up to tend to him.

When I awaken again the sun is up and, as usual, I find him curled on
the kitchen floor. He has left the back door ajar and the cat has found him;
she lay curled next to his legs with her chin resting on his ankle. As is my
habit, the first thing I do is open his knapsack and pull out his journal. Its
leather cover was new and shiny when he left here five weeks ago, and its
pages were crisp and empty. Now it is ragged and smudged, filled with
drawings and verses and stains.

His road journal contains the distinctive scribbles of the wry, gentle,
home-body I know him to be. Most of his verses are filled with longing: he
pines for me and for the comforts of home and hearth. But another man also
appears in those pages, a lonesome tramp whose voice is only familiar to
me in these writings, one who must wander the earth and capture its subtle
riches as some catch and collect butterflies. For instance, some of the verses
recount his drinking bouts with a hermit who lives in a cave overlooking a
perilous ravine. I do not know this man who drinks sake with hermits until
he passes out and awakens startled from nightmares of tumbling into the
abyss; this is not my husband. And, for the third time now in as many years,

there are some verses about a certain nobleman's wife who lives on a hilltop overlooking an orchard. She is often left alone because of her husband's many duties in the city. He describes her voice in the song of the nightingale. He depicts her cheeks in the vivid cherry blossoms. He sees her long hair in the eddies of the river during spring thaw. This, also, is not my husband; I have never met this creature.

It is my habit to spend the days following his journey painting what he has written. When I paint the nobleman's wife, it is always her back I paint, as she reaches for fruit beyond her grasp, her face in profile, partially covered by her flowing hair. My husband, the one I know so well, the one who has shared my bed for thirty years, seems satisfied by these poses. When I read these verses, I wonder that he still returns to me. She seems so much younger and prettier than I. Perhaps one day he will leave me and never return. Perhaps there is no perhaps about it. Whether the nobleman's wife is to blame or not, such a day is coming — the day my beloved disappears over the mountain and I never again feel the warmth of his embrace.

When his eyes open, I am sitting at the kitchen table, turning pages. "There is a sunset somewhere in there," he says, pointing to the journal, "that burned as bright in its final moments as any I have seen. I'm not sure my words have captured it. It filled me with a sense of dread," he says, "as though it were the final sunset, as though our days had come to an end and we would have only the moon's pale glow to guide us from now on. During the night I awoke several times feeling that my breath was being stolen. I thought it must be a sign. But finally the sun rose like any other day. The birds sang. The breeze warmed. It was a sign only of my foolishness. Do you mind being married to such a fool?"

"I will try to paint it," I say.

"Paint the fool or paint the sunset?"

"The fool and his sunset."

"I wish I had been given the gift of painting, like you."

"I will trade you my pictures for your words."

"Too late for that. We are both of us too far down our respective paths to turn back now."

He looks up at me the way he always does on the mornings of his return, as if he adores me, as if I were the wisest and most beautiful woman in the world. In these moments the other man in his pages, the one who drinks too much sake and visits lonely married women, is eclipsed by the husband who devotes himself to his own wife and his own modest home. It is this husband I cling to during the nights after my own terrifying sunsets.

I spend most of the morning cutting his matted hair, shaving him, soaking the stench of the road from his dungarees, and stitching up his torn knapsack. If his verses are to be believed, he made it all the way to the ocean this time. The beginning and the end of his journal are filled with the usual mountain images. But the middle is filled with the screeching of seagulls, brine on the breeze, the pounding of waves against rocks, sand crabs, and moonlight on the water. I will gladly paint these things, for I've grown weary of pine branches and stars, jagged mountain peaks, lonely bobcats, and crickets — always crickets.

I feed him a cut cucumber from the garden and a jug of fresh water from our well. I bring out the new paintings I've made while he was gone — Cypress branches in moon light, cherry blossoms along the river bank. He rubs his chin and cocks his head as he examines them. He closes one eye and holds each canvas at arm's length. He nods and purses his lips. He takes my right hand, the one I hold the paintbrush with, and kisses it as if it is the hand of a lovely princess who has granted him pardon for all his secret crimes.

He walks onto the back porch and fills his pockets with wheat germ pellets from the bucket. He ambles out to the bridge over the pond, drops the morsels one by one into the gaping mouths of the koi. How like those fish I am, straining for his attention each time he returns, taking each morsel and opening wide for more. When the wind cools and the clouds gather over the gazebo, he comes inside and stokes the kitchen fire with fresh coal.

I have drawn his bath. He loves to sit upright in the deep tub, piping hot water up to his neck. He sits like a statue until the water cools. When I hear him soap up, splash off, and pull the drain, I prepare his chaise lounge on the back porch. He likes to sit under a blanket after his bath and sip a cold beer and watch the birds flit around the Cypress tree that overhangs the pond. Today he whistles to them and calls them by name before he dozes off. He snores for about an hour before he stirs. During this time I prepare our tea.

When my sister visited last year she laughed at our rituals. "You are like a pair of monks," she said, "with your long silences and your ceremonial teas. You should go out once in awhile. Why not have some friends over for a dinner party?" Her husband is a businessman; she herself is a school administrator. For her, a simple life devoted to beauty is nonsense. "We are made for more than scribbling and painting," she likes to say.

As the clouds darken and roll ominously across the late afternoon sky, our neighbors trim the ornamental trees in their yard; the snip-snip of the hedge trimmers adds a rhythmic counterpoint to my husband's snoring. Finally he rises, grunts, stretches until his fingers touch the underside of the back porch awning. He walks across the bridge and relieves himself against the fence at the edge of our property. I can hear his farts all the way in the kitchen. The cat peers into the pond, then follows him back to the house like a dutiful disciple.

I carry the tray out onto the porch. It has begun to rain. The cat prances into the house and curls up on the futon. My husband kneels and bows. We sit across from each other, the tea tray between us, and listen to the rain. There are few things in this world more lovely than the sound of rain on the pond, on the gravel, on the awning above our porch. My husband once said that in all his travels he has never seen a garden so fragrant and beautiful, at once spare and lush.

I scoop the powdered tea into my grandmother's bowl. As I pour in the hot water and stir it with the whisk, it makes a green froth. I bow my head as I lift the steaming bowl to his lips. He accepts it and sips with eyes closed. When he opens them, he smiles, and his face blossoms with beatific wrinkles and worn, crooked teeth. There are moments when the familiar beauty of my husband's weathered cheeks and nose and lips and ears and neck become too much for me, and I must glance at the sky to clear my head.

When I turn my gaze back to him, he is studying my face — my cheeks, nose, lips, ears, neck— and I feel the blood warm my face.

In his contentment, I find contentment. My sister insists this is not possible. She believes my love is only weakness, my heart a slave's heart. She has never loved, never known love. She can't begin to imagine giving herself wholly to another. In her mind, love is a delusion, a dream we give ourselves over to in order to make a harsh, ugly world bearable. When my husband is gone, I am almost convinced that she is right. But when he returns, I know that all will be well, and in his presence all is well.

He wipes the lip of the bowl with the linen cloth. He lifts the bowl to my lips and I, too, sip with eyes closed, savoring the sweetness of the matcha. I have never yet painted him. I have told myself that when he fails to return, then I will paint him. If he were gone, I could still count on my hands and my mind to place him in the center of the canvas. I have studied his face enough to render it in a few simple strokes. I will put him in his road clothes, with his staff and his knapsack. I will paint stubble on his chin. His head will be cocked just so, for he will be listening to the crickets. His eyes will look toward the horizon, beyond the mountains, to a blazing sunset.

Later he sits on the futon next to the cat, opens his journal, lights his pipe, and begins the long work of editing. In a few weeks time, these jottings will be shaped into a fine book of poems that he will dedicate to me. I go into bed and lie down for a nap. I awaken a while later to darkness, the sound of rain against the bedroom window, and the smell of dinner on the stove. The house is steamy and fragrant. I slip on my favorite robe, the one with a peacock on the back. I shuffle out to the kitchen and see that the table is set, the wine is poured. The cat is in the corner eating a few fresh scraps he has separated out for her. She is so happy she purrs loudly while she eats.

The window brightens suddenly with a flash of lightening. A few seconds later, thunder rumbles and crackles. When the lightening flashes again, I can see the rain bouncing off the top of the fence outside. The thunder is closer now, and the windows rattle. The cat has moved under the table. She will spend the evening rubbing against our legs but she will not allow us to pick her up.

Dinner is always the same on the day of his return. Our traditional feast begins with hot and sour soup, followed by jasmine rice (the valley floor), mushrooms (the forest floor), fried pork (the mountains), halibut (the sea), bok choy (the valley again), and ends with mint ice cream. Afterwards, he reads to me from Basho. I read to him a sermon from Soseki. The wine has warmed his cheeks and loosened his tongue. He begins to narrate for me his passage along the river, his encounter with a leprous fisherman who fed him and let him sleep in his barn; he describes the owl who shared the loft with him but whom he refused to render in verse. "Some things," he says, "I must keep for myself." He wipes his lips with his napkin, adding hastily, "And for you, of course. This creature would only have been belittled by my words."

As he is talking I am lulled by the sound of his voice and by the sound of the receding thunder. They merge momentarily. I begin to see myself wandering the house without him. A flash of lightening illuminates his staff, which leans against the fence in the pouring rain. In that instant it appears to have bloomed, producing bright pink blossoms up and down the staff. Where has the cat gone? I hear her scratching at the back door. In another lightening flash the house is momentarily transformed into a ruin, with no ceiling; it is a skeleton of decayed and crumbling walls. The sound of the cat scratching at the door calls me back to reality, back into my husband's presence. He yawns as he finishes his story about how the owl brought him a vole in the night, and how my husband ate it raw, with gratitude.

"This rain won't last," he says. "Morning will be bright and fresh. The birds will wake us early." He gets up and walks into the bedroom. The image of my husband eating the rodent the owl brought him is difficult to shake. Some part of him is beyond my comprehension, beyond my reach. It is the part of him my sister described as "primitive" on the day of our wedding, as she was twisting my hair into a thick braid. It was her last attempt to dissuade me from the marriage, I think, only an hour before the ceremony. She had asked me to explain what I felt for him. But as I spoke I could tell by her expression in the mirror that I would never get through to her. Taking a clip from her mouth and pinning the braid atop my head, she had said in a pinched voice, "I suppose he does have a certain primitive energy."

As I am rinsing the dishes, I look out into the garden. The lightening has subsided. I cannot see his walking staff. I trust that it is leaning against the fence in its usual spot. I trust that it has not actually sprouted blossoms, pink or otherwise, and that it will be there, in another few months or so, when he grows restless, fills his knapsack, kisses me on the forehead, the nose, the lips, plucks the staff from its place one summer afternoon, and walks towards the mountains.

The kitchen stove has grown cool. I rinse my mouth with the last of the wine. I open the door for the cat. She stands there sniffing the air for a moment, then decides to remain indoors. The clouds have split apart, revealing the gibbous moon and a few bright stars. When I have said my piece to them, I lock the door and pull down the shades. I take down my hair and I go into him, letting my robe fall to the cold slate floor. He has opened the window, as is his habit, and the moonlight falls across our bed. The sheets are cool and crisp. The air is charged with the freshness that follows such storms. My husband is home. Do you hear me? My husband is home. ∎

Which Nazi Are You?

DEAR GRANDPA,

I have never met you but once you sent a box to our house at Christmastime with a bunch of nuts and fruit and cheese in it. Do you remember doing that? I ask because my mom says your memory is lousy after a lifetime of soaking your brain in rum. The only thing I know about rum is Johnny Depp drinks it, and it makes him brave. Does it have the same effect on you? Do you look like Johnny Depp? My brother says we are related to Johnny Depp as well as you. How about that? — two famous movie stars in the same family.

But about your memory mom says like, for instance, you forgot to show up for half her life as a little girl. She gets very extreme when she talks about you. Her cheeks and her ears turn red. Lately there's a vein that pops up on the side of her neck, and it like throbs when she starts to think about you. If she were a girl in the Twilight stories, she would be the first victim. If you were a teen vampire, could you resist that juicy vein just bulging with fresh blood?

I'm writing to you because I watched *Raiders of the Lost Ark* last week and my Aunt Hanna told me you played one of the evil Nazi soldiers. You guys were like really scary. My friend Ella says *Raiders* is very old school and not really scary at all. Not like *Saw* or *Playback*, which are both rated R and definitely not for kids, but her dad lets her watch R movies when she stays at his house, even though it makes her mom boil over when he does that. Ella says *Raiders* is no way as good an action flick as *Fast and Furious*. I haven't seen *Fast and Furious* but my brother Troy likes it, too. My brother Troy likes a lot of things I don't. Troy says you can't beat *Fast and Furious* for action.

But even though *Raiders* was made many decades ago and is boring in parts, I don't personally think it's old school. Ella's dad used to be a TV producer before he opened his car lot and so Ella talks like she's the authority on all things Hollywood. But Ella can be dead wrong about things and this is one of them. I don't think your movie is old school. I was totally caught up in the chase scenes and even some of the talking parts, which are usually boring but not always. But it was definitely the chase scenes that kept the movie going.

I didn't actually know what a Nazi was when I saw this movie but my Aunt Hanna explained that they were the bad guys in a war that I haven't studied yet but will probably get to sometime in high school. I feel like I learned a bit about the Nazis already from this movie. Even though their uniforms are dull, just plain brown, they have the most interesting accents in the movie and certainly the most energy. I especially liked the truck chase scene where the Nazis are climbing all over the truck and punching Indy and trying to throw him off the truck.

So my question is: which Nazi are you? Because the movie is like crawling with Nazis. Everywhere you turn there are men in brown shirts. My mom knows, or says she knows which one is you, but she refuses to watch *Raiders* because you're in it. She says it makes her hurl. Aunt Hanna doesn't even know for sure which Nazi you are because she was little when you left for Arizona. Whenever I mention it my mom says something like, *He can goose-step himself straight into the mouth of hell for all I care.* She doesn't want to discuss you and she doesn't want me to talk to you — ever. She doesn't know I'm writing this, and if she knew she'd do something drastic, so please don't tell her.

She's mad about her and Reggie's break up. Reggie is our step-dad and he has left the building as they say. Reggie and mom had a huge fight about money and when the fight about money ended it became a fight about Reggie's drinking, which is not something my mom can abide. That's the way she talks sometimes. She says, *I can forgive a multitude of sins but drinking I cannot abide,* like that. I think she inherited some of your acting talent because sometimes she talks like she's in a movie. Not an action movie but one of the ones with all the talking in it.

Anyway, she says she grew up with a miserable alcoholic for a father and she refuses to be married to one. She says she doesn't want to live in a goddamn Tennessee Williams play. My brother Troy has a theory that her whole world is whacked because when you left the building her soul was possessed by the devil. Up until that point you were protecting her because you were religious and had a guardian angel at your side, even though you were an alcoholic. Are you still religious? We have no religion in our house. Ella's mom is married to a very religious man now and he has a statue of the Virgin Mary in Ella's backyard.

I'm not sure what this has to do with anything except to say that my mom is a very unhappy person since Reggie left. It's like he was her guardian angel and now she's possessed again. That's my brother's theory anyway. My brother is full of theories. For instance, he believes that the president of the United States is an alien disguised to look human. It's this whole big story he has about how aliens from another planet have like slowly and secretly taken over our planet and little by little they are making it more like their home planet. So that's my brother for you. But I think he's right about our mom's anger all the time, especially now that Reggie has left the building. I'm not sure about the devil part, but what do I know?

So lately I've been sort of wondering if you might maybe think about making up with her? Don't get mad at me for saying so, but I think her being mad at you is making her mad at everybody. That's not my brother's theory, that one is mine. Whatever you did to make her mad happened a long time ago, right? Maybe you don't even remember what made her mad. So maybe now that all this time has passed you could just, you know, be the grown-up and apologize. Aunt Hanna says this to mom all the time. *It's time for you to be the grown-up, Mary Lou.* Even though Aunt Hanna is younger than my mom, she talks like she's the big sister. Aunt Hanna is mad at mom because she married Reggie on the rebound. Reggie is not much of a grown-up either according to Aunt Hanna on account of his gambling addiction.

Reggie just plays the horses, mom says. You can't be addicted to horses, can you? I love horses. Whenever Reggie takes us to Los Alamitos racetrack he walks us down to see the horses while he talks to the jockeys. The jockeys are friends of his. So Reggie talks to the jockeys while my brother Troy and I pet the horses. I guess I won't be petting horses anymore now that Reggie has left the building.

Aunt Hanna says don't say this to your mother but Reggie looks a little like a short Nazi. Aunt Hanna says the head Nazi had a mustache and Reggie has a mustache, too. I don't remember any of the Nazis being short, but it's hard to tell how tall or short anybody is in the movies. Ella says that sometimes the tall actors stand in a ditch so they'll be the right height for the scene. Sometimes they stand on a stool. For instance, she says Tom Cruise is constantly standing on a stool in his movies since in real life he's only about four feet tall. She has this on authority from her father, who sold Tom Cruise a car once.

My brother, by the way, says he remembers you. Is that possible? Sometimes he makes things up and pretends they're true. I can usually tell the difference between the made up stuff and the true things. With this I can't tell. He says you came to our apartment when we lived in Redondo Beach. This was before Reggie. After my dad died and before Reggie moved in. Maybe you didn't even hear about my dad dying. He may have been murdered, we don't know. It's an unsolved case. He disappeared and then his body was found floating in one of the canals near Belmont Shore. It was this whole big thing on the news. I miss him like crazy. He used to take me to the beach a lot. We used to ride the waves on our boogie board before it broke in two. Troy says it's damaging for children not to have a male role model in the house. Now we are three-time losers, he says, because you are gone, our dad is gone, and now Reggie is gone.

Anyway, Troy says you brought us presents that day you came to Redondo Beach and mom threw the presents out into the street. Does this sound like something you might remember? He says mom began lighting matches and throwing them at you. I don't think he made this up because of the whole match thing. Who could just pull something like that out of the air? I was maybe taking a nap or staying with Aunt Hanna at the time because I have no memory of this and my brother says I wasn't around. So even though he saw you that time he doesn't know which Nazi you are either. He says all Nazis look alike to him. I don't think like that. My brother is my brother and I am me. I looked closely at the faces of the Nazis and they all look different. I mean, they're all still bad guys and such — with all the same brown costumes. But each Nazi has a different face.

I have so many questions I'd like to ask you. For instance, what was it like to drive so fast in the Nazi truck? Troy says you are only going like ten miles and hour and they speed up the film to make it look fast. But it looks to me like your truck is kicking up enough dust to be actually speeding across the desert. I dreamed once that I was driving fast. It was easily the best dream I ever had. I'm not anywhere near old enough to drive, but I was driving in my dream, racing down the boulevard that goes to the beach. And when I got to the beach the car I was driving became a speedboat. What was really weird but also awesome was that my dad was there in the boat with me. This was about a year after he died. And I was like, Dad? And he was just sitting there while I was driving. He was watching the waves. He didn't talk. We drove all the way across the ocean to Catalina Island, just me and my dad.

When I woke up I felt sad again, like I did the day they showed his body on the evening news. You couldn't see his body because it was covered with a tarp, but you could see that it was a body laying next to the water, and the news guy said my dad's name. I'd like to dream that dream again. I want to go back, like they do sometimes in movies. I've tried to climb back inside that dream, hoping that maybe I'll think enough to say something, to get him to talk to me, like he used to. But dreams don't work like that.

Anyway, I guess I'm rambling. My mom is always shushing me. Aunt Hanna calls me her chatterbox. Aunt Hanna used the word "estranged" to describe our situation. Is that a word you know? I looked it up but the definition seems fuzzy. I think what she means is that you are a stranger to us. Like if I saw you at the mall or something, I'd walk right past you without knowing you were my grandpa, much less one of the Nazis in *Raiders of the Lost Ark*. My sincere wish is that we will all be destranged — or is it unstranged?

It's not so weird that we were estranged in the first place. All my friends have somebody in their family that is estranged. Nowadays, says Aunt Hanna, it's basically an epidemic. It's not something they talk about in random conversations, but practically everybody has an estranged relative in their family tree. Just ask people you know and they'll tell you. Since you are more or less the trunk of our family tree, this is a fairly big deal. As you can see, I've been thinking a lot about this.

My point is — maybe now that Reggie has left the building — maybe now would be a good time for you to drive out here and be the grown-up. My name is Carol, by the way, in case you don't know or don't remember. And according to my Aunt Hanna I'm your granddaughter. She gave me your email address after I asked her to search you down on-line. I hope this really is your email and not some random person. Think how weird it would be to get this email out of the blue. Aunt Hanna says she's not sure it's you. She says there's a chance that you might be dead. That would be sad — sad for me and Troy and sad for Aunt Hanna who says it's time to bury old hatchets, but really sad for my mom, who may never stop being mad. I'd hate for her to soak her brain in rum because of this old hatchet.

Well, even if you don't come to visit us, I just wanted you to know that I'm not like mad at you. My mom gets mad but that doesn't mean I have to. I am my own person, and I think it's hella cool that you were in *Raiders of the Lost Ark*. Aunt Hanna says you were in other movies, too. Ones they don't show anymore. So all I'm saying is maybe someday they'll show them again, and then maybe you won't feel like you need to soak your brain in rum.

I have asked Aunt Hanna to also find me Johnny Depp's email. She says she's still working on it. I know it's a long-shot because Troy says Johnny Depp lives even farther away than Arizona, in one of the countries the actual Nazis marched into, and he would not want to be bothered by random relatives. But I figure since I'm at it, why not try and reconnect all of the branches back to the trunk?

Sincerely,

Your Granddaughter (Carol) ∎

About the Author

DAVID DENNY is the author of *Man Overboard* (Wipf & Stock), *Fool in the Attic* (Aldrich Press), and *Plebeian on the Front Porch* (Finishing Line Press). His stories and poems have appeared in numerous journals, including *Atlanta Review, California Quarterly, Pearl, New Ohio Review,* and *The Sun.* He holds a Master of Fine Arts (M.F.A.) degree in creative writing from the University of Oregon and a Master of  Arts in Theology (M.A.T.) degree from Fuller Theological Seminary. Recent honors include an Artist Laureate Award by the Arts Council of Silicon Valley, a two-year term as inaugural Poet Laureate of Cupertino, California, and numerous Pushcart nominations. Denny is Professor of English at De Anza College and former editor of *Bottomfish* magazine. He lives in the San Francisco Bay Area with his wife Jill, a prominent choral conductor and music teacher. They are the proud parents of two talented children and the timorous guardians of a persnickety cat named Molly Bloom. When not writing or teaching, Denny can often be found watching classic movies from the balcony of the Stanford Theatre in Palo Alto.

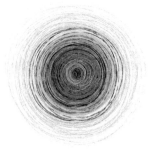

ART · NATURE · SPIRIT

SHANTI ARTS celebrates art, nature, and spirit through exhibitions and publications. If you enjoyed this book and would like to find out about our other books, we invite you to visit us online. There you will find a complete list of our books and serial publications as well as information about exhibitions, artist and writer opportunities, and book submissions. Our books may be purchased on our website, through most online booksellers, and at many fine bookstores.

If you would like to receive mailings about our exhibitions and publications, please visit our website and add your name to our mailing list.

shantiarts.com
info@shantiarts.com

CPSIA information can be obtained at www.ICGtesting.com
Printed in the USA
BVOW11s1534071215

429599BV00011B/100/P